LIGHTS OUT

8:15 p.m.
It's a hot summer night in Boston, and the sun has just set. The sky is a royal blue canvas against which the city skyline shines.

8:45 p.m.
Lighted boats glisten in the harbor, tourists gather under the twinkling lights and colonial streetlamps glow along old cobblestone streets.

9:00 p.m.
Jewels sparkle on the necks of world dignitaries partying at the Hancock Tower penthouse. Princess Ariana dances in the arms of exciting, enticing Shane Peters, whose ebony eyes gleam in the candlelight. Night has settled gently over Boston…

9:10 p.m.
…until the blackout hits.

As the city plunges into total darkness, only one man knows the reason why. The man who aims to wreak the revenge he's sought for a decade.

And only he knows how far he'll go to get it…

Dear Reader,

I was really excited when I was asked to write the first book in the LIGHTS OUT continuity for the Harlequin Intrigue line. It's a fabulous story—with a great suspense thread running through all four books.

One thing I love about writing continuities is that I get a chance to work characters and plots I wouldn't have come up with on my own.

The heroine of *Royal Lockdown* is Princess Ariana LeBron of Beau Pays, a small European country. In a million years, I would not have chosen a princess for a heroine. But I took on the challenge and had a lot of fun getting her to loosen up and enjoy what security expert Shane Peters has to offer. He's just the type of hero I like to write. Strong, capable, confident and sexy. He's got a hidden agenda at the diplomatic reception where he meets Ariana. But will he trip himself up royally? And can he save their lives when the going gets downright dangerous?

For my next Harlequin Intrigue book, I'm back to 43 LIGHT STREET, with a hero who acquires supernatural powers when he opens an antique box. It's like a genie in the bottle—only in reverse. And I'm looking forward to writing it.

Best wishes,

Rebecca York, aka Ruth Glick

REBECCA YORK

ROYAL LOCKDOWN

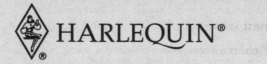

HARLEQUIN®

TORONTO • NEW YORK • LONDON
AMSTERDAM • PARIS • SYDNEY • HAMBURG
STOCKHOLM • ATHENS • TOKYO • MILAN • MADRID
PRAGUE • WARSAW • BUDAPEST • AUCKLAND

Special thanks and acknowledgment are given to
Rebecca York for her contribution to the
LIGHTS OUT miniseries.

ISBN-13: 978-0-373-69261-3
ISBN-10:   0-373-69261-7

ROYAL LOCKDOWN

ABOUT THE AUTHOR

Award-winning, bestselling novelist Ruth Glick, who writes as Rebecca York, is the author of close to eighty books, including her popular 43 Light Street series for the Harlequin Intrigue line. Ruth says she has the best job in the world. Not only does she get paid for telling stories, but she's also an author of twelve cookbooks. Ruth and her husband, Norman, travel frequently, researching locales for her novels and searching out new dishes for her cookbooks.

Books by Rebecca York

HARLEQUIN INTRIGUE
717—INTIMATE STRANGERS*
745—THE BOYS IN BLUE
    "JORDAN"
765—OUT OF NOWHERE*
783—UNDERCOVER ENCOUNTER
828—SPELLBOUND
885—RILEY'S RETRIBUTION
912—THE SECRET NIGHT*
946—CHAIN REACTION
994—ROYAL LOCKDOWN

*43 Light Street

Don't miss any of our special offers. Write to us at the following address for information on our newest releases.

Harlequin Reader Service
U.S.: 3010 Walden Ave., P.O. Box 1325, Buffalo, NY 14269
Canadian: P.O. Box 609, Fort Erie, Ont. L2A 5X3

CAST OF CHARACTERS

Shane Peters—As soon as the lights went out, the security expert went on high alert.

Princess Ariana LeBron of Beau Pays—She came to Boston to attend a diplomatic reception and ended up trapped in a terrorist attack.

Charlie Mercer—Did the president's Secret Service agent do his job?

Ty Jones—The Secret Service agent couldn't keep the vice president from being kidnapped.

Chase Vickers—He was stuck in his limousine, out of the action. How could he help?

King Frederick of Beau Pays—He'd sent his daughter to Boston. Now he was sick with worry.

Liam Shea—Would he get his revenge tonight?

Colin Shea—He'd stop at nothing to kill Shane Peters and the princess.

President Stack—He showed his true colors as the commander in chief.

Vice President Grant Davis—Was the past coming back to haunt him?

FBI special agent Ben Parker—Did he steer Shane and Ariana wrong?

FBI special agent Harold Wolf—They left him in charge of a mess. How was he going to save the situation?

Prologue

He could never get his life back. His good name. His career. But in just a few hours, he would exact his revenge against the man who had stolen everything from him. Or men. He had never been sure which of them had sandbagged him on that ill-fated rescue mission.

Tonight it didn't matter who was the chief culprit. They would all suffer, for being in the wrong place at the wrong time. Just the way it had happened to him on that long ago night when disaster had struck.

First he would scare the spit out of them. Then he would take away everything they held dear, like stripping the flesh off their bones. And when they were on their knees, bleeding and begging for mercy, he would give them mercy. He would end their miserable lives.

The law wouldn't call it justice. But he had long ago given up his faith in the American justice system. If you wanted retribution, you had to go out and do it yourself.

He'd been humiliated in public and tossed in the slammer for a crime he hadn't committed. And his wife hadn't even stood by him. Either she'd believed the lies they'd told about him, or she hadn't been able to take the guilt by association.

Right after he'd been convicted, Margaret had started divorce proceedings and tried to wipe out any vestige of their marriage from her life.

They'd had three sons together. But she'd changed his boys' last names and moved them far, far away, where he could never contact them.

Poor humiliated Margaret had lived for five years in Oregon, then she'd died of uterine cancer. He figured that was God's retribution.

And the beginning of hope for him. Without her around to constantly poison their minds, the boys had gotten back into contact with their father.

Now they were a family again. More than a family. A well-disciplined covert unit.

Without his sons, his plans for this night of terror would be impossible to carry out. But the boys were all in place, all ready to execute their roles in the drama that was about to unfold.

He had been out of prison for a year, making plans and setting up the conditions he needed. He looked at his watch. Eight ten. He had a little less than an hour before the show started.

His pulse was pounding, just as in the old days before a mission. Only this one was his creation. You could even think of it as performance art.

He had timed everything carefully. He had gotten his body into fighting shape with sessions at the gym and on the winding roads outside of town. He might be eleven years older than when they'd tossed him in the slammer, but he could keep up with his sons on a five-mile run carrying a ten-pound pack. And he could rappel down the side of a sixty-story building, if he needed to.

This sixty-story building.

He turned his head to the right and looked out the expansive windows at the panorama spread below him. From his vantage point, he studied the twinkling lights of the city. He could see the spire of Trinity Church. And Old South Church. And the skyscrapers that had sprung up in the downtown area.

It wasn't quite dark yet on this summer night, but already Boston was relying on artificial light.

Not for long.

Smiling, he turned away from the window. Just getting into this secure location had been a major victory. Now it was time to don the uniform that would make him virtually invisible when the mission started.

He was leaving nothing to chance. Once again he began methodically checking the kit that held his equipment.

Making a list and checking it twice, he thought with a grin as he lightly touched one of the automatic weapons he'd stowed in a sports bag. But he wasn't Santa Claus. Far from it.

He pulled out his gas mask and made sure it was ready to go over his face when he needed it. He checked the focus on his night-vision goggles.

Then he went on to the hostage kit, starting with the duct tape and ending with the hypodermic needles.

Everything was ready. Now all he had to do was wait for dark.

Chapter One

"May I see your picture ID, sir?"

The armed man made the request politely. But Shane Peters harbored no illusions about what would happen if he refused. He'd be hauled off to a cell in a Boston police station and held for investigation.

"Of course," he answered as he pulled his wallet from an inside pocket of his tuxedo jacket and extracted his driver's license.

The Secret Service agent checked the ID carefully, then asked for his Social Security number, which was matched against a list of guests cleared to attend the reception on the observation deck of the John Hancock Tower, New England's tallest building.

Since 9/11, the Boston landmark had been closed to the public. But one of the lessees had been instrumental in arranging an international trade agreement that had just been signed by the president of the United States. Tonight the observation floor was open for a reception in honor of the agreement, and guests had come from all over the world.

To commemorate the momentous occasion, President Stack and Vice President Davis would both be attending the event. Of course, that was highly unusual, since protocol dictated that they remain in separate locations as much as possible. But they would only be together on site briefly.

Because of the unprecedented joint appearance, the Secret Service had gone into overdrive on background checks for everyone scheduled to be in the tower—from the honored guests to the waiters and kitchen staff.

The line to pass through security moved slowly. Shane watched some of the formally dressed men and women being ushered through the metal detector. He knew that in his custom-tailored tuxedo, he could pass for a member of the upper classes. But he was also aware that men and women with any security experience tended to mark him down as "dangerous." So he wasn't surprised when he was singled out for the wanding treatment.

He struggled to stand cooperatively as he let the guy do his job. Too bad he knew the drill better than the man wielding the wand.

Shane owned his own high-powered company called Executive Security. That much was on the public record. But that was only the tip of the iceberg. He was also a member of Eclipse, an elite force that took on jobs too sensitive for the FBI or the CIA.

He and the other members of Eclipse had all met in the Special Forces. Most of them would be here tonight, although only some of them were actually on duty.

They hadn't been on a mission together in several months, and Shane was looking forward to seeing the guys. Of course, if they knew what "Wild Man Peters" was up to tonight, they'd haul him off to the funny farm before he made it into the reception room.

He repressed a grin as the guard sent him on his way—without even checking the special pocket sewn under the arm of his tuxedo jacket. Sewing wasn't one of his favorite skills, but he'd made the modifications himself, to keep the alteration secret.

He waited at the elevator, then rode upstairs with a nice selection of the rich and famous. Most of them had the look of confidence and well-being that money brought. It amused Shane to think that he could buy and sell most of them.

Between his security business and Eclipse, he'd made all the money he was ever going to need. He could retire to his very comfortable underground mansion in the White Mountains and keep busy with his electronics inventions. But inventor was only a small part of his job description. He was too restless to work in the lab every day.

Instead he thrived on challenges—like the one he'd set for himself tonight.

The elevator stopped at the sixtieth floor, and the glittering crowd exited, ready to party. Before they were permitted to enter the reception room, they were treated to a second security check.

Although some of the guests muttered about being stopped again, Shane had been expecting it.

This time one of the Secret Service agents recognized him and let him step through the metal detector. Instead, the agent singled out a balding insurance executive for the wand treatment.

After clearing the metal detector, Shane stepped aside to let another couple hurry past, then strode toward the reception hall, where candles flickered in the center of white linen tablecloths. At the edge of the room, floor-to-ceiling windows gave a view of the city lights. The windows were part of the reflective glass skin that covered the whole building. Shane remembered that early in the life of the building, a number of them had fallen out and crashed to the sidewalk.

Note to self—stay away from the windows.

"Champagne, sir?"

"Thank you." He accepted a flute from one of the formally clad waiters. But after taking a sip, he set the glass down on one of the tray stands scattered around the sides of the room. Right now he needed a clear head. Later he could celebrate with some bubbly.

The reception hall was already fairly crowded, and he recognized dignitaries from countries as diverse as China and France. He looked around to see if he could spot King Frederick of Beau Pays. He'd been happy to see the king's name on the guest list. Before Frederick LeBron had taken the throne of his small Alpine country, he'd pursued a variety of interests. He'd earned several advanced degrees from the Sorbonne, in Paris, then made a point of taking some top-secret political and military jobs, just like a regular working spook. He'd been the translator on a hostage rescue mission to the Middle East with Shane, the men who now made up Eclipse and three other highly trained operatives.

The mission had blown up in their faces when one of the members had jumped the gun and gone in too soon. Luckily, they'd gotten most of the hostages out alive, although three had died, including the U.S. secretary of state.

Wishing he hadn't flashed on the gory details of that

long-ago mission, Shane swiftly tried to rearrange his features into a more party-like alignment.

But thinking of LeBron had brought back disturbing mental images from the past.

Shane felt a cold chill ripple over his skin. Suddenly, with terrible certainty, he knew that something bad was going to happen here tonight.

As soon as the thought surfaced, he firmly shoved it out of his mind. He was nervous about his private plans for the evening. That was all.

Or was fate telling him that he'd better abort the harebrained scheme before he got into serious trouble?

He usually listened to his sixth sense. Now he cursed his unexpected attack of nerves.

Sorry that he'd put down the champagne flute, he looked around the room and spotted Ty Jones over by the French doors to the balcony.

The man was six feet tall. At two hundred pounds, he was fit and muscular, not a bodybuilder, just a Secret Service agent who stayed in shape.

As usual, his blond hair was falling across his forehead.

Ty's gaze swept the crowd, checking for anything or anyone that looked out of place. When he spotted Shane, they smiled at each other. Ty was one of the Eclipse team. But his day job was with the Secret Service, and he was with the vice president's security detail. Which either meant that the VP was already on site or would be soon.

When Ty went back to his surveillance assignment, Shane crossed to the special display that had been set up before any guests had arrived at the reception.

In a heavy Lucite case, guarded with a silent alarm,

was the priceless Beau Pays sapphire that the first king of the small Alpine country had given his wife on their wedding day.

As Shane looked down at the ninety-carat gem, which was twice the size of the Hope Diamond, a man came up beside him. Shane recognized him as Preston Hyatt, an oil-company executive who was known for his own collection of fabulous gems.

"That thing should be under armed guard," Hyatt commented. "If it belonged to me, I wouldn't loan it out for a trade reception."

"Yeah," Shane agreed.

"I guess it's got state-of-the-art security," the man murmured.

"Uh-huh," Shane answered, repressing a secret grin.

Supposedly the security system guarding the gem was flawless. But he'd used his covert skills to get up here earlier, and he knew that the precautions the guards from Beau Pays had taken were laughable—at least in the face of one of his newer inventions, a bypass system that would fool the alarm into thinking the protective grid was still in force.

Hyatt drifted away, and Shane stood for several seconds contemplating the gem—until the feeling of being watched made him turn. He expected to see one of the security men zeroing in on the case with the sapphire. Instead, a porcelain-skinned beauty in a gown that matched the sapphire-blue of the gem was staring at him from across the room.

He took in details like a camera snapping shots in rapid succession. Her hair was light blond and worn in an upsweep, decorated with a gold tiara as delicate as her features. Her eyes were light blue or green. He couldn't tell the exact color from this distance. She was small and slender, yet the way she stood, tall and straight, gave her a regal bearing.

The crowd of people around him dimmed to a blur. Suddenly he felt as if he'd stepped from the reception room into the middle of a dream.

What was that line from the old Broadway musical? Something about seeing a stranger from across a crowded room. And knowing that person was *the one*.

He felt as if a hundred-pound hammer had thunked him in the chest. His heart skipped a beat, then started up again in double time.

It was several heartbeats before he remembered to breathe, several seconds before his brain engaged again. When it did, one thought surfaced. He wanted to be alone with this woman in a bedroom, although the sudden lustful ache was nothing compared to the emotions flooding through him.

In the next moment, his memory for names and faces clicked into place. He'd never met her in person, but he knew who she was—and knew that he didn't have a chance in hell of being anything more than her casual acquaintance.

Princess Ariana LeBron was off-limits to the likes of Shane Peters.

ARIANA LEBRON STOOD stock-still, struggling to keep her face from revealing any emotion as she stared at the tall, lean-bodied man on the other side of the room.

He was devastating in formal attire. She suspected he'd be just as appealing in a pair of faded jeans, T-shirt and scuffed loafers.

His shiny black hair was styled to perfection. His

eyes were dark, too, and focused on her with a laser intensity that tied her stomach into an instant knot.

His name was Shane Peters. She knew that from her recent research.

To aid her in identifying the foreign dignitaries and others attending the reception, the State Department had supplied her with an annotated guest list. As she'd crossed the Atlantic in her private jet, she'd read up on many of the men and women who would be attending. Being prepared for any situation went with the job of heir to the throne of Beau Pays.

As she'd studied the information, she'd been especially interested in Shane Peters because her father had talked about him on more than one occasion. He was ex-Special Forces. A security expert. And also an inventor of specialized electronics equipment.

Of all the pictures she'd looked at on the plane, his had stopped her. He'd intrigued her. She'd taken in his sinfully long lashes, his ebony eyes, his perfect white teeth. Now she knew that the photograph had been a pale shadow of the flesh-and-blood man.

She could see that there was more to Shane Peters than a biography and the photo he'd slapped onto the information sheet about his company. An aura of danger surrounded him, and she knew instinctively that he'd be a bad man to have on the opposing side of any fight.

Which was one good reason for staying away from him, she reminded herself. Another was the pull she felt when she stared at him. He was a brash American, just the wrong sort of man for her. She couldn't date a man simply because she was attracted to him. Duty to her people and to her country came first.

Since her brother, Rolf, had died in a skiing accident

four years ago, she was the heir to the throne. And since she would be thirty in two months, she'd selected a suitable fiancé from among the nobility of her country.

His name was Jean Claude Belmont, and he would inherit a dukedom. She had thought of practicality, not love, when making her selection.

From observing her own parents' polite and friendly marriage, she knew that love was just a fairy tale. You picked a mate because he fulfilled certain purposes. Like Jean Claude, who had a Ph.D. in government. He would father her children and give her advice when she needed his counsel.

He was home now, attending a meeting she'd had to skip to come here—a meeting of the committee setting up a program where poor women in her country could get free day care for their children while they entered job-training programs and then went out into the workforce.

But when her father's gout had flared up, he'd asked her to attend this reception in his place. And she hadn't refused because duty had been drummed into her since she was a child.

Still, for just a moment, she let herself wonder what it would be like to go off alone with a man like Shane Peters. What it would be like to let her hair down and do anything she wanted.

"Is something wrong, Your Highness?"

She blinked, coming out of her reverie and ruthlessly snapping off the fantasy. Turning to her bodyguard, Manfred, she flashed a brilliant smile.

"No. I was just admiring the Beau Pays sapphire," she said, smoothly disguising her state of mind.

"Yes. It looks stunning," Manfred agreed. "The centerpiece of the reception."

"As it should be," she murmured, then took a slow, calming breath as she looked around the room, taking in the richly dressed men and women. The Americans, she noticed, tended to overdo the glamour scene, and the women often showed too much flesh in their choice of attire.

As she and Manfred talked, she couldn't stop herself from looking for Shane Peters in the crowd. He appeared to be circulating around the room, talking easily to people he knew. But she could tell he was keeping her in his sights.

Well, she knew he was brash. What did he think— that they were going to slip off into some private room together?

She felt her skin heat as she realized she'd been having exactly that thought. The wrong thought.

Or did she have an excuse for talking to the man? After all, he'd been on that mission with her father. That gave them something in common. And maybe he could fill her in on some of the details from that long-ago night that she'd never been able to get her father to talk about.

Still, the back of her neck prickled as she watched the security expert circle toward her, making it look as if she weren't in his radar at all. But as a princess, she had a lot of experience reading people.

Well, she didn't like being stalked. Maybe she could leave before he made his move. Right after the president made his little speech, she'd go back to her room at the Ritz-Carlton to study the Women's Workshop proposal.

She felt herself wavering again. The indecision wasn't like her.

Lifting her head, she turned away from Peters, looking for one of the waiters circulating through the room. One glass of champagne wouldn't hurt, she decided.

Just as she found one of the servers and took a step forward, the lights flickered, then went out.

Chapter Two

In the darkness, some of the guests gasped. Others laughed nervously. To Shane's amusement, the ambassador from Wintonia began shouting something belligerent about American incompetence.

"What's going on?"

"Turn on the lights."

"This isn't funny."

"Is it a terrorist attack?" a woman whispered to the man beside her.

The large reception room had turned into a shadowy cavern, except for the radiance of the moon shining through the floor-to-ceiling windows and the candles flickering on the linen-clad tables.

Shane cursed under his breath, remembering his earlier premonition. In the sudden darkness, he felt naked without a gun in his hand. But it would have been impossible to get into the reception with a weapon.

He'd already marked the location of Ariana LeBron and her bodyguard, a guy named Manfred Werner. Shane started toward them, shouldering his way through the immobilized party guests, just as the lights flicked back on again.

People blinked in the suddenly renewed brightness as gasps and nervous comments were replaced by sighs of relief.

Shane found the princess and her muscular body-guard and was relieved to see that the brawny man was doing his job. He had moved her into a corner where she wouldn't get trampled if people suddenly started to panic.

With the light level back to normal, a murmur of conversation and questions had started up in the room. Everybody, including Shane, wanted to know what had happened. To find out, he needed inside informa-tion—or outside information, depending on how you thought about it.

He saw his friend Ben Parker across the room and wove his way through the crowd toward the FBI agent.

Parker looked as if he was staring into space, but Shane knew he was listening to a transmission through his earpiece. Hopefully, his government sources were telling him what had caused the momentary blackout, and he'd be willing to share the information with a friend.

When Parker appeared to be ready for a live con-versation, Shane asked, "What was that business with the lights?"

The agent's expression turned disparaging. "Just the usual summer problems with Boston Power and Light. They need to update some of their equipment."

"No chance of a repeat?"

"The mayor and the president of the power company don't think so."

"You guys still going to allow both the president and the vice president to be here?"

"We've got it under control," Parker bit out.

"Thanks," Shane answered, still on edge, but thinking the momentary blackout had given him a perfect opportunity. Everybody was focusing on what had just happened. They wouldn't be thinking about the Beau Pays sapphire at the moment.

ARIANA FELT MANFRED SHIFT his position. He'd curved his body around hers earlier and now he straightened, tugging at his jacket.

"Thank you," she murmured.

She knew the physical contact had made him uncomfortable, but she also knew he'd been doing his job.

"Do you think that happens often in the United States?" she asked.

"I hope not. But this is summer, and the Americans love their air-conditioning. There's more drain than usual on the power system."

"Was it just this building, do you think?"

"It was the whole city," Manfred answered immediately. "I looked out the window and saw all the lights go out. There was nothing illuminated as far as the eye can see, except the motor-vehicle headlights and some boats in the harbor."

She shuddered. From her research, she knew that the population of Boston was six hundred thousand, and the metro area was much bigger. How far had the blackout extended? And what had happened during the moments of blackness?

Was the crisis a good enough excuse for her to slip out of the reception now? Couldn't she cite security concerns?

Even as she asked the question, she silently admitted that her disappearance would be conspicuous. The news would surely get back to her father. He'd sent her all the way across the Atlantic to attend this reception, and he'd be disappointed in her if she slipped out so soon. Once again, she was reminded of her duty.

Just as she finished the internal debate, the orchestra began playing "Hail to the Chief." Even if she'd wanted to leave, it was too late now. Like everyone else in the reception hall, she turned toward the double doors that led to the elevators, watching the tall, salt-and-pepper-haired man stride in.

In her royal role, she'd met many heads of state, and she saw instantly that President Stack had the presence of a ruler. Vice President Davis was also quite impressive, standing with the straight posture of a military man.

"Thank you for coming, especially those of you who have traveled here from outside the United States," the president said.

"I believe the new international trade agreement that our countries have signed is a good step toward global cooperation. Whether we like it or not, we've entered the era of a global economy. And helping that economy run smoothly benefits every nation of the world, no matter how large or how small.

"I'd like to especially welcome some of our distinguished guests."

He named the British secretary of commerce, the French foreign minister and then looked in her direction.

"And we're particularly honored to have Princess Ariana of Beau Pays with us this evening."

She gave him a gracious smile, then turned to acknowledge the applause that filled the room, glad that she hadn't ducked out before this moment. She didn't love being singled out, but she understood that her royal status added cachet to the occasion. Many of the people here would go home and talk about meeting her, even if they'd been no closer than the other side of the room.

She was happy that the president had specifically mentioned her country's participation in the agreement. Beau Pays might be small, but her father and her grandfather had made a point of cooperating in treaties and initiatives that would benefit the world community.

Her training allowed her to pretend that she didn't mind the extra attention the other guests were giving her. Yet she couldn't shrug off an unsettling feeling that prickled at the back of her neck. The feeling that someone in the room did not wish her well.

Beside her, Manfred was scanning the formally clad men and women, and she suspected he was picking up the same vibes that she had. Was there someone here who had a bone to pick with Beau Pays?

Perhaps now was the time to leave.

She was about to tell Manfred to alert their driver when a movement in the crowd made her glance up to find Shane Peters striding toward her, looking inordinately pleased with himself, she noted.

As he stopped in front of her, she felt Manfred tense and knew that she had to defuse the situation at once before her bodyguard took the man out in the hallway and demanded to know why he was getting so close to his charge.

Smoothly, she gestured toward the newcomer. "Manfred, this is Shane Peters, an old friend of my father's."

Peters didn't miss a beat. "I came over to introduce myself, but it seems you've been reading my bio."

"Yes, I recognize you from your dossier," she answered, deliberately making it sound as if there were a secret file on the man. Up close he was even more devastatingly handsome than he had been from across the room, and she wanted to put some distance between them. If not physical distance, then emotional distance.

Really, the "dossier" contained only general information of the sort she'd found on the other people who would be here tonight.

"I hope you enjoyed reading about my checkered career."

She refused to take the bait.

A more polite man would have understood what she was doing and backed off. In this brief encounter she had already learned that Shane Peters didn't necessarily observe the social niceties.

He kept his gaze on her, and she had to remind herself to breathe calmly in and out.

"I was hoping to see your father here."

"He was indisposed. He sent me in his place."

Peters's face clouded with what looked like genuine concern. "I hope he's all right."

"It's nothing serious," she quickly assured him. Gout was painful but not life threatening. Her father was back on his special diet now and medication that would diminish the attack.

"Good." Peters gave her a smile that must have melted many female hearts. "We should dance."

"Dance?" As she spoke the question, she realized that the orchestra had begun to play a waltz. It was one of her favorites. "The Blue Danube."

Peters opened his hands, as though inviting her to step into his embrace. "To celebrate the trade agreement," he said.

The invitation was very tempting, but she knew on a deeply personal level that she shouldn't accept. She was also aware that Manfred was watching the exchange with interest. He had been with her for the past three years, and he knew how she always behaved in public.

True to form, she gave Peters her standard answer. "I prefer to stay on the sidelines."

"One dance won't hurt you, will it?" the American pressed. Obviously he didn't know anything about royal protocol.

She wanted to tell him that he'd already disturbed her equanimity enough for one evening, but that would give away far too much.

So she thought of another way to create distance between them, to take them away from this place and time, at least temporarily.

"My father met you on a rescue mission, right?"

"Yes. In Barik. It's near Libya."

"I know where it is."

"Sorry. I should have realized you're a lot better educated than the average American who probably hasn't even heard of the place."

She acknowledged the apology, then turned the conversation away from herself again. "My father is an expert in Middle Eastern languages."

"I always wondered why," Peters answered without missing a beat.

"Because he said that the Middle East would emerge as a center of power in the world and he wanted to be prepared."

"Very wise of him. And of course, his being able to speak Arabic helps him in negotiating for oil."

She smiled. "That, too." Before he could get too far into economic issues, she brought the conversation back to the topic that interested her. "Tell me about the mission."

"What did your father say about it?" Peters countered.

"He said that you went in to rescue a group of fifty-eight hostages, mostly engineers, teachers and missionaries, who were being held in the basement of a building in the densely populated downtown area. The captives were from the U.S., England, Australia and Beau Pays."

Peters's face took on a faraway look, and she knew that, in some sense, he was back there in that civil war-torn country reliving the night he'd been dropped off by helicopter in the capital city.

"They were held for weeks in horrible conditions. The world prayed for their safety, but the country was becoming more and more unstable, with insurgents fighting the government and fighting each other. The captors kept up negotiations, but they seemed to be getting nowhere. Finally, the only option was a rescue mission."

"Who else was on the team?"

"Chase Vickers was our engineering expert. Ethan Matalon was our computer ace. Ty Jones was our demolitions man. And, of course, Vice President Davis was our tactical expert."

"You keep in touch with them?"

"Well, I haven't seen the vice president in years. But the others are still my friends. Chase is a driver who gets a lot of jobs working for VIPs when they're in town. Ty is right over there." He gestured with his hand.

"He's with the Secret Service guarding the vice president. A very prestigious assignment."

"You and the others got the hostages out of there."

"Most of them," he answered, and she caught a flash of pain on his face. There were aspects of the mission that her father never talked about, and it looked as if she wouldn't get a straight story from Peters, either. Something, she knew, had gone terribly wrong. But what?

Peters was silent for several moments. Then, before she realized what was happening, he reached out and touched her hand.

She wasn't sure why he'd done it. To change the subject? To break through the barrier that she'd tried to erect between them? All she knew was that she felt a jolt of sensation like an electric shock going through her body.

Her breath caught, and when she looked into his eyes, he appeared to be as stunned as she was.

Life had taught her to be a realist. She knew a lot of men wanted to be seen with her because she was Princess Ariana, the heir to the throne of Beau Pays.

But this man looked as if he was reacting to her on a very personal level.

He was attracted to her. And she had the honesty to admit that she was attracted to him as well.

So what would be the harm of one dance? They weren't going to see each other after tonight. She'd be safely home tomorrow. And safely married six months after that.

"Let's dance," she whispered.

Manfred looked startled and started to say something, but she shook her head, and he closed his mouth.

But obviously he would report this incident to King Frederick.

"Watch my purse," she said to him as she set it down on one of the tables.

He nodded curtly.

Yes, he would speak to her father. And if the king chastised her, she could always fall back on the excuse that she was being nice to one of his old friends.

She let Peters lead her to the dance floor. She already knew that the two of them had nothing in common beyond the man's long-ago mission with her father. In the span of a waltz, she'd find out that they really had nothing to say to each other, and she could walk away from him without regret.

But she didn't have to walk away yet. Not when he had taken her in his arms and pulled her to him so that her body touched his.

She liked the way the man held her. The way he smelled—a combination of masculine skin and some woodsy scent she couldn't identify. And she liked the way his large hand splayed across her back, his fingers grazing the line where her evening gown dipped along her backbone.

She realized with a start that she was enjoying the proximity entirely too much. She should take a step back and put some distance between them. Instead she stayed where she was as he began to move her around the floor.

He was an excellent dancer, and if he'd been anyone else, she could have relaxed in his arms and let him guide her smoothly through the waltz steps.

But with proximity came tingling awareness spreading through her bloodstream. She tried her best to ignore the sensation. Yet when he gathered her closer and stared down into her eyes, she had to fight a swirl of unaccustomed emotions.

A look of pure, burning sexuality passed between them. No man of her acquaintance would have dared to be so bold. Which only proved that she didn't belong in Shane Peters's arms. He must have had a lot of sexual experience. She had virtually none, because as the princess of Beau Pays, she was expected to maintain high standards of decorum. She had never stepped over the line—not even with Jean Claude.

ONE OF THE WAITERS STOPPED for a minute and stared at the couples circling on the dance floor.

He saw Shane Peters and the little blond princess from Beau Pays. Automatically, he noted their location, then told himself not to bother. By the time he needed to find them again, they'd be long gone from that part of the floor.

But he'd find them. There was no doubt in his mind.

He stepped from the reception room into the kitchen area, put down the empty tray he'd been carrying and looked at his watch.

Almost time to go into action.

Around him, a dozen staffers were busy doing their jobs. Most of them worked for the catering company. But others had been added to the roster because the party was large.

Everyone here tonight had undergone a rigorous security check, given the high-level guest list. Still, his fake credentials had held up perfectly. As had those of the three other men working with him.

One of them gave him a quick look and put down his own tray.

Unfortunately, the waitstaff manager noticed that two of his workers were slacking off.

Striding across the room, he demanded, "Where do you think you're going?"

"On break."

"You're not scheduled for a break."

"Sorry." The imposter strove to keep his voice even. "Come over here. I want to show you something."

"What?"

"I can't describe it. You have to see it for yourself. It's right over here."

Walking purposefully, he led the manager into an alcove off the service area where the staff bathrooms were located, then grabbed the man by the hair, tipped back his head and slashed a knife across his throat.

The assault was over in seconds. Before the imposter could drag the manager into a closet, an unfortunate kitchen worker chose that moment to step out of the bathroom.

When he saw the tuxedo-clad man lying in a pool of blood on the tile floor, he gasped and tried to jump back into the safety of the men's room. But another one of the conspirators was already on him, taking him out like the first victim.

The first victim. It felt good to think those words.

The night's real mission had begun. And before the sun rose, there would be a lot of important names added to the victims list.

Two more bogus waiters joined the men who had stepped into the alcove. They dragged the dead men into the bathroom and dumped them by the urinals.

They also retrieved the bags with their automatic weapons, night-vision goggles and gas masks from the bottom of the waste bins.

Then, by mutual agreement, they turned to the

mirror and began to remove the disguises they'd been wearing. One pulled off his glasses and mustache. The other tossed into the trash bin his false nose, cheek pads and the appliance that changed the shape of his mouth.

As soon as they were back in the hallway, the other two men disappeared into the bathroom and performed similar operations—quietly and efficiently, the way they had practiced.

Soon all four of them were standing in the hallway—Uzis in hand—waiting for the signal.

The youngest of the conspirators shifted his weight from one foot to the other. "How much longer before we make our move?"

The man who had dispatched the catering manager gave him an indulgent look.

"Any minute now." The speaker made an effort to sound calm, but he could hear the tension in his own voice, could feel adrenaline coursing through his bloodstream. They had planned carefully for this night. They had taken every contingency into consideration. Now they were ready—as soon as they got the order to move out.

If any other unfortunate employee had to go to the bathroom before the mission went down, then he'd end up like the two men already lying dead on the floor.

SHANE WAS USED TO GETTING what he wanted. He had wanted to dance with Ariana LeBron and now she was in his arms. But he found he wanted far more than one or two dances. He knew he was letting a fantasy carry him away. The heir to the Beau Pays throne wasn't going to get involved with a guy who'd been raised in a series of foster homes.

Even in the U.S., where you were supposed to be able to improve your station in life by talent and hard work, he still felt like an outsider in a group like this. Even if he didn't *look* like an outsider.

In Europe, he knew things were different. If you were born on the wrong side of the tracks, you didn't end up getting cozy with royalty.

But tonight he wasn't going to bow to convention. He'd pulled off a damn slick coup a few minutes ago, and he was going to celebrate his success by enjoying the woman in his arms.

She was so delicate, so beautiful, and she had a sharp mind. He always liked that in a bed partner.

Bed partner!

In your dreams, Peters.

"Have you seen the Danube?" she asked.

The question threw him, and he struggled to bring it into context. Then the music registered on him. "The Blue Danube" waltz.

"Yes. I saw the river when I was in Vienna. And Bratislava."

"Not many Westerners have visited Bratislava."

"I was on an assignment." He didn't elaborate, since he'd been working for Eclipse, shutting down a weapons-smuggling operation that had ferried former Soviet armaments from Prague to Austria where they'd found their way to various terrorist groups in Western Europe.

He couldn't talk about that, or any of his Eclipse missions, so he circled back to her original question. "I was disappointed to see that the river was more gray than blue. Of course, that might be different in summer."

Just then, Shane felt a buzzing sensation and thought

for a moment that it came from his reaction to Ariana. Then he realized he was feeling the vibration of his cell phone. A text message was coming in, and he should take a look at it.

But he wasn't here on business. At least not anybody's business besides his own. So he ignored the phone and let himself drift on the buzzing sensations in his brain, sensations created by the woman in his arms.

He'd inched her closer to him, so that his cheek was pressed to hers. Her delicate skin felt wonderful against his face, and if the dance floor had been less crowded, he would have closed his eyes, the better to concentrate on the feel of her body, her scent, the small hand that rested on his shoulder.

Over the years, he had enjoyed the company of many women. But he had never let a relationship knock him off his pins. Tonight, though, he was having trouble breathing and thinking straight as he held Ariana LeBron in his arms.

Some part of his mind shouted that this was the wrong woman for him. The wrong time. The wrong place. He was crazy to be thinking of starting anything with her.

Yet his mind kept zinging back to that electric moment when they'd first touched. From her shocked expression, he knew he hadn't been the only one who'd felt that thrill of discovery.

She could have backed away from him then, but she'd joined him on the dance floor. He knew that she could have easily put some distance between them. Instead she allowed him to press her body against his as they moved in time to the music. It flitted through his thoughts that she might be having the same problems as he was.

His mind ventured further into forbidden territory. Could you go to jail for kissing a princess?

Probably. But that wouldn't happen unless she made a fuss later. And if he kissed her, he'd make sure she had nothing to complain about.

He looked around the reception room, seeing men and women enjoying themselves. Polite enjoyment. Nothing you couldn't show on the late news this evening.

He, on the other hand, was going up in flames on the dance floor.

So was there any chance in hell of getting her off alone, without that muscle-bound bodyguard hovering over them?

To do what? Steal a few kisses? That wouldn't be enough. Not hardly. But he'd probably have to settle for mouth-to-mouth intimacy.

He stopped thinking about the wisdom of his decision as he moved them across the dance floor, putting as many couples as possible between Ariana and the hulking Manfred.

He looked toward the balcony. If they went out there, they'd be alone. Of course, the huge windows were a problem. But if they moved around the corner, they'd be blocked by a wall.

He had almost reached his goal when the lights flickered out again.

Ariana straightened and drew in a small breath.

"They came back on last time," she whispered.

"Yeah. Give it a minute," he said reassuringly, hoping that this was another false alarm.

He waited with his heart pounding inside his chest. When the lights stayed out, he knew that the first flickering of the electricity had only been a warning of worse to come.

Because *this* was the disaster he had sensed was coming his way when he'd first stepped into the reception hall.

Chapter Three

Maybe this was just another snafu on the part of Boston Power and Light. Or maybe it wasn't.

Regardless, the blackout was an instant security nightmare.

Shane wondered what FBI agent Ben Parker was thinking now. He'd been so sure that everything was under control when the lights had come back on. At the moment, he must be struggling for bladder control.

Shane looked at the foreign dignitaries around him, now visible only in shadow. With President Stack and Vice President Davis in attendance, the building, he knew, would be on lockdown. Nobody was going in or out until the Secret Service said it was safe to move.

Unless it turned out there was some hidden danger right here in this room. Like a bomb.

Various scenarios flashed through his mind as he instinctively moved to protect the woman in his arms.

He inclined his head so that his mouth was against her ear. "We have to get out of the middle of the floor."

"Yes."

Obviously she'd had disaster training, and she made no protest as he led her toward the side of the dance floor.

She turned her head to say in a low voice, "I've got to get back to Manfred."

"Not yet. It's too dangerous to move around until we know what's going on and how the people here react."

She raised her head, and he saw her taking in the room and the suddenly darkened world beyond the Hancock Tower.

"What happened?" she asked.

"Last time, it was a minor problem at the power company," he answered. He didn't want to alarm Ariana, but he'd had a bad feeling about this reception, and he wished he'd paid attention to his instincts.

At the moment, his gut was telling him that the blackout wasn't the result of faulty power-company equipment. The emergency was focused on this building. This event.

Nervous chatter had broken out among the guests at the party, and Shane was pretty sure that the Secret Service had already gotten the president and vice president into a secure location.

But he recognized the symptoms of panic and knew the crowd was on the verge of chaos. As if to prove the point, one of the female guests started screaming.

"Stop it!" a man shouted.

Ignoring him, she broke away from the crowd and ran toward the balcony doors.

"Dora, come back," her companion ordered, then rushed after her.

Still too panicked, she flung the doors open and dashed outside.

"You have to get her back in," Ariana whispered. "Before she does something…dangerous."

Shane was torn. He wanted to stay by the princess,

in case the formally dressed men and women here turned into a mob. Before he was forced to make a decision, Secret Service agents grabbed the escapee and dragged her back inside.

One of the agents raised his voice. "Everybody, stay cool. We have the situation under control."

Let's hope so, Shane muttered to himself. .

In the flickering light from one of the candles, Shane recognized a tall man standing near him. It was another one of the agents who had earlier spread out through the crowd. "Shane Peters, from Executive Security," he said, as though he were on assignment here and not just one of the guests. "I have Princess Ariana LeBron with me. Can you give me a status report?"

"My communications networks say that the blackout has hit the entire city," the man said. "And many of the suburban areas."

"I think it's focused on this reception," Shane answered, pitching his voice low so as not to further alarm anybody nearby.

"How could that be? The whole city's involved," the man snapped.

"It's a diversionary tactic," Shane answered. "And it keeps rescue operations from zeroing in on us."

"Interesting scenario," the agent said, then took several steps away, cutting off the conversation and signaling what he thought of Shane's theory.

Shane swallowed the curse that rose to his lips. It made him furious when people who should know better had tunnel vision.

Next to him, Ariana shuddered, and he turned his attention back to her. "You think we're under attack?" she whispered.

He stroked a hand slowly along her arm, feeling the goose bumps that peppered her skin. They hadn't been there a few minutes ago. "I hope not. But I think we have to act that way. Stay with me."

"All right."

Reaching down, he linked his fingers with hers. Her hand was even colder than her arm, and he gave her a reassuring squeeze.

"We have to get out of here," she murmured.

He signaled his regret by the tone of his voice. "I don't think we can. The building's no doubt on lockdown."

She sucked in a strangled breath. "How long do we have to stay in this room?"

"Until the power comes back on. But believe me, it's not any safer outside the building. There'll be cars stuck, traffic jams, road rage, looters and people going berserk because they're terrified that this is another terrorist attack."

Her voice turned high and strained. "Do you think it is a terrorist attack?"

"I don't know," he answered honestly.

As if to confirm his grim assessment of the situation, the sound of several car horns drifted toward them from the street, followed by the sound of a gunshot.

Ariana shuddered. "That was a gun."

"Yes."

She kept her face straight ahead and spoke in a low voice. "Are you armed?"

He suppressed a frustrated sound. "I wish I were. But I couldn't get through security with a weapon."

"So you're not on duty tonight."

"No. I'm just a guest."

Before he could make another comment, his phone vibrated again, reminding him that he'd received a text message earlier and had ignored it because he'd been too focused on Ariana.

Pulling out his phone, he flipped up the top and read the message.

Are you afraid of the dark?

"What is it?" Ariana asked. "Something to do with the blackout?"

"I think so."

Ariana tipped the phone toward her and read the message. "What does that mean?" she asked.

"I don't know."

"No other messages?" she asked sharply.

He shook his head and grimaced in the darkness. "My phone vibrated while we were dancing. I ignored it."

She could have come back with the comment that he should have been tending to business. But before she could say anything, the door to the kitchen opened with a loud thud.

Everybody in the room turned toward the sound. In the flickering glow from the candlelight, they could see that four tuxedoed men had entered the room and slammed the door behind them to draw attention to their presence.

When one of them briefly turned on a flashlight, everybody in the room saw that he and his companions were armed with assault weapons and night-vision goggles.

"All of you into the center of the room!" he shouted, his voice a grating command.

Instead of obeying, people went stock-still. Stunned silence was followed by a babble of voices.

Once again, the man's command cut through the noise. "Into the center of the room if you don't want to get hurt!"

Frozen in place, Ariana whispered, *"Mon Dieu."*

Shane shared the sentiment, but he had no intention of letting her be herded into a central location, since he had no idea what the men with assault weapons intended.

"Come on," he whispered.

They were in the wrong part of the room to try for the main entrance, and the gunmen were blocking the kitchen door. But he had another idea.

Taking Ariana's hand again, he lost no time in tugging her away from the crowd and toward a space he'd found when he'd searched the room last night.

It was a slot in the wall where room dividers had once been folded when not in use. The dividers had been removed from the reception area, but the slot remained, and Shane hoped to hell it would make a good hiding place.

As he moved Ariana swiftly through the crowd, he could imagine what Ty Jones and the other Secret Service agents were doing right now. Could they get the president and vice president out of the reception area? Or were they stuck with his method of hiding and hoping for the best?

One more question about Ty circled in Shane's mind. Had his old friend gotten the same text message? *Are you afraid of the dark?*

Various scenarios raged through his thoughts as the armed men ruthlessly herded the guests into the center of the room.

Shouts of "Move it!" and "Hurry up," were accompanied by hard shoves.

When an older man stumbled, one of the assailants kicked him and ordered him onto his feet.

"My heart," the victim shouted.

"Quiet! Move."

The man scrambled up, and Shane wondered if the guy was going to make it out of the room alive—whether or not the bad guys shot him.

Who were these guys, anyway? And how had they gotten past the tight security and into the reception?

His mind flashed to the waitstaff that had earlier been passing champagne and canapés. Had these four men come in with the catering company? On the face of it, the plan seemed damned ballsy. But he knew that these thugs had done something few men would attempt at a reception attended by both the president and the vice president of the United States.

They must have been up here previously casing the tower. With part of his mind, Shane wondered what would have happened if he'd run into them yesterday.

That was then and this was now.

In the darkness, Shane kept moving, pulling Ariana away from the center of the action. Yet he couldn't keep a tiny doubt from creeping into his mind. Was he going the right way or turned around in the dark?

What if he was actually putting Ariana in more danger?

He led her along the wall, praying that he knew where he was going.

His tension grew as the seconds ticked by and he didn't come to the slot in the wall. Then finally his fingers brushed against the edge of the hiding place he'd discovered yesterday. Breathing out a small sigh, he stopped short.

"Right here," he whispered as he moved Ariana into

the narrow opening in the wall, hoping that the dark would hide them when the assailants did a thorough search of the room, which they surely would as soon as they had better control over the crowd.

He followed Ariana into the opening, then turned to face the middle of the room again. One of the armed men was shouting another order to the formally dressed herd. "Put out the candles on the table."

Nobody moved.

In the next second, a burst of automatic-weapons fire split the air. One of the male guests went down, groaning. Shouts and screams erupted throughout the reception area.

"It's the ambassador from Wintonia," someone gasped out. "He needs a doctor."

"Leave him!" The order came from the captor who was directing the action.

Behind Shane, Ariana made a gagging sound. Shane turned and cupped her head, pressing her face against his chest as he stroked her back. She was trembling, but he felt her struggling to control herself.

"We'll be okay," he whispered.

Although she nodded against his chest, he wondered if she really believed him. More important, did he believe it himself?

"Hang tight," he murmured.

"I'm trying."

He gathered her closer, cradling her delicate body in his arms. "Pretend we're still dancing."

"Oh sure."

Because he knew it would distract her, he said, "I kept hoping I could get you off by yourself. I wasn't looking for this particular excuse."

"I knew you were thinking about it," she answered.

He nuzzled his lips against the top of her head. "So what would you like to do with me?"

"I'm too well trained to tell you my fantasies."

"You should learn to go with the flow."

The banter helped temporarily, until the gunman-in-chief issued another order.

"Shut up and put out the candles before I take out someone else."

Shane turned halfway around so that he could see the room.

This time, people scrambled frantically to obey, and the room went from candlelit to gloomy. Now the only light came from the moon.

A woman went down on her knees beside the ambassador.

"He's dead. You killed him," she sobbed.

"Quiet. Or you'll be dead, too," one of the armed men barked out.

The woman tried to muffle her sobs as a man lifted her up and pulled her away, but Shane could still hear her weeping. He wondered if she was going to survive the night. Or if he and Ariana would, for that matter.

"Hands up. Nobody move."

Obedient in their fright, everybody in the center of the room raised their hands and stood still.

Shane could only see shadows now, but he imagined the men with the night-vision goggles looking like figures out of a horror movie.

"I'm speaking to the Secret Service now," the chief gunman said. "Three people have already been killed. Take out your weapons and put them on the floor or more innocent people will die. If you want that on your heads, then stand there like dummies."

Nobody spoke. The only sound in the room was the whisper of sidearms being drawn from concealed holsters.

As he strained his eyes and listened, Shane assessed his chances of acquiring one of those weapons. Not good. Not when the opposition could see the room perfectly, and he had only moonlight to guide him in a room full of frightened people who were ready to go into panic mode.

A few moments ago they had been happily celebrating an international trade agreement. Now they were living their worst nightmare.

"Okay. Now, to the Secret Service and everybody else, take out your cell phones, walkie-talkies, any other communication devices. Drop them."

Again, the crowd obeyed. He heard cell phones hitting the floor all over the room. He still had his own phone—for all the good it did him. The authorities must know what was going on at the top of the Hancock Tower. If they could mount a rescue attempt, they would.

On the other hand, maybe he'd be able to give the police some information. He could always dial 911. Or he could contact his brother, Chase, who might be downstairs in one of the limousines parked along the curb. But he couldn't risk making a call until he got Ariana out of the reception room.

He turned back to her, gathering her close, and he realized that she had stopped trembling.

When he shifted his stance, she raised her head. *"Je suis bien."*

He knew she wasn't really okay. But she was showing her royal training and her moral fiber. How many women would have remembered to reassure the guy in hiding with her?

"Uh-huh," he whispered. She had to be scared out of her mind, but at least the darkness had spared her the sight of the ambassador getting killed. Or maybe the darkness had made it worse.

His mind scrambled frantically for a plan that would keep her safe.

The men out there were obviously ruthless. Obviously willing to kill to get what they wanted. And he didn't even know what that was yet. The sounds outside their hiding place told him the captors were gathering up the discarded weapons and cell phones.

A man in the crowd voiced Shane's thoughts. "What do you want?"

None of the captors spoke. Instead, the question was answered with a burst of gunfire. Another one of the guests screamed and fell to the ground, and Ariana cringed.

"Steady," he whispered.

Outside their hiding place, something else was happening. Again he turned, and movement in the reception area riveted his attention. Two of the captors were silently and slowly moving around the walls, checking for anybody who hadn't followed directions and gathered in the center of the room.

He felt his jaw muscles clench. Had he pulled Ariana into a death trap?

Praying that their hiding place would be undetectable, Shane quickly drew the princess farther back into the niche in the wall. When he came to the recess where the mechanism for the folding walls had been removed, he eased her into the tiny space, then followed her inside. It was a tight squeeze, and he had to hold her against his body so that her breasts were crushed against his chest.

Her breath was shallow, and he wanted to say something reassuring, but he'd run out of quips. Besides, talking was no longer an option with the gunman so close.

As footsteps came toward them, he felt Ariana tense. The fight-or-flight reaction.

His own muscles were strung as tightly as coiled springs, but he knew there was little an unarmed man could do when he was standing twenty feet away from an assailant with an itchy finger on the trigger of a submachine gun. A man who had already killed much too casually.

Maybe the only advantage Shane had was surprise. From an inside pocket in his tuxedo jacket, he withdrew a small folding knife. Designed to pass through a metal detector, it was made of very thin plastic. He opened it and held it in his hand, prepared to slash at the gunman if he got the chance. It was a pitiful strategy, but his only option at the moment.

As the footsteps came toward them, he prepared to spring. The man stopped at the niche in the wall, and Shane pictured him staring inside, his night-vision goggles giving him an excellent view of the narrow space. He wondered if his tuxedo jacket was sticking out. Or maybe his shoe. He wanted to inch closer to Ariana, but he knew that any movement would be a fatal mistake. So he stood there with his breath frozen in his lungs.

The man took a step into the crevice, and Shane almost whirled and lunged with the knife.

Gritting his teeth, he held his breath and forced himself to keep cool. After seconds that felt like centuries, he heard the man take a step back, then another. But he remained in front of their hiding place for what seemed like eons. Finally, he moved on, and Shane let the breath trickle out of his lungs.

He heard Ariana doing the same.

"All secure," one of the armed men reported to his leader.

That's what you think, you bastard.

Ariana's fingers dug into the arm of his tuxedo jacket. "Hang in there," he whispered.

"What do they want?" she asked, her voice wispy.

"I'm sure we'll find out soon," he answered in the same barely audible voice.

"This could be like that school in Russia. Did the captives ever know why they were being held?"

"Maybe not," he conceded.

He'd like to think this was about money. Or power. He suspected the motive was going to be a lot worse.

He felt Ariana shift her body. "Could you give me a little breathing room?" she whispered.

"Of course."

He needed some breathing room himself. On the dance floor, he'd been all wrapped up in the intimacy of holding her so close. Now the proximity was only adding to his uneasy feeling.

He needed to clear his head and think. Reluctantly, he stepped away from her and took a breath.

"I'll be right back," he whispered.

"Where are you going?" she asked quickly, tension quivering in her voice.

He gave her arm a quick squeeze. "Not far. To see if

I can find out what's going on. Stay here—you'll be okay."

Quietly he walked to the front of the crevice, then he got down on his hands and knees.

Round tables with long white skirts were scattered around the room, and he used one of them to shield himself as he tried to get a better handle on the situation.

Out in the reception room, one of the captors spoke again. He'd put on a gas mask, which muffled his voice. But the message was all too clear.

"There is no escape from the reception area. If you try to leave, you will activate our fail safe system, releasing cyanide gas into the room. Everyone here will die, except for the four of us who are equipped with gas masks."

Cyanide gas.

As the words assaulted Shane, he felt a shudder go through his body. And not just because he knew the effects of the deadly poison. He remembered once before when he'd been in a dangerous situation and cyanide gas had been an important part of the equation. It was on that long-ago mission to Barik when everything had suddenly gone bad.

Oh, Lord. Was that what tonight was all about?

It couldn't be. Yet even as he tried to downplay the importance of this new element, he was thinking about the man on the team he hadn't mentioned to Ariana.

Liam Shea had been one of the players. And he was the reason the mission had turned from a smooth-running covert operation into a horror show.

After they'd gone in, Shea was supposed to wait for a visual signal, but he'd reacted too fast. He'd cut the power to the complex before the rest of the team had been ready. His premature action had resulted in the death of the U.S. secretary of state and some innocent citizens.

He'd been court-martialed, dishonorably discharged and sent to jail for the screwup, though he'd maintained all along that someone had given him the visual signal.

Because methodical habits had saved Shane's life more than once, he had kept tabs on Shea over the years. Not that he'd thought the man was going to come after him. Still, he knew exactly when Shea had gotten out of prison.

And he knew that the jailbird hadn't stayed around. He'd gone underground almost as soon as the prison gates had closed behind him.

Shane had thought it was because he was no longer equipped to function in society. Now he wondered if Shea had had big plans that he hadn't wanted to reveal.

Was he back now, out for the sickest kind of revenge his twisted mind could conceive?

Shane crawled to his right and craned his neck, trying to get a good look at the leader of the men who had set up this terrifyingly well-executed scenario.

He couldn't tell if it was Liam Shea. In the goggles and gas mask the man was unidentifiable.

Plus, Shane hadn't seen Shea in years. On the mission the man had been one of the older members. Then he'd been locked away, which had probably sped up his aging. Shane wondered if he'd even recognize Shea.

Shea had insisted all along that he was innocent, but the court hadn't believed him. So was this the desperate act of an innocent man who had decided the only way he'd get justice was through revenge?

If so, who were the men with him?

He'd had three sons, Shane remembered. Could he have convinced them to go along with his revenge plot? Were they so loyal to their father that they were willing to kill for him?

Of course, that brought up a whole other issue. If Liam Shea had really been innocent, who had made him the fall guy for the failed rescue attempt?

There had been eight men on the mission, although one of them—Commander Tom Bradley—was dead now.

The four who had joined Shane in Eclipse were above suspicion. He would trust any one of them with his life.

Yet a lot of them were here tonight, he suddenly realized, as he put the evening into a different context.

Chase might be outside in one of the limousines. Ty was guarding the vice president. Only Ethan was absent. But Shane knew he was in Boston, suffering in the same blackout as the rest of them. Maybe he was frantically trying to protect his young son from dangers Shane could only imagine.

Another man who had been on the mission was Vice President Grant Davis. He was here tonight, too. The eighth member of the team, King Frederick of Beau Pays, was absent, but his daughter was standing in for him tonight.

Maybe they'd all been brought here on purpose. And maybe that would work to Shane's advantage.

Perhaps he and Ty could do something if they could link up…

Shane balled his hands into fists. He was getting way ahead of himself. This wasn't an Eclipse operation.

There might be a room full of people at risk, but Ty had to focus on his primary duty: protecting Vice President Davis.

Hopefully, he'd already gotten Davis out of the building.

Which meant that Shane was on his own.

Chapter Four

Enjoying his position of power, Liam Shea stared at the crowd of frightened men and women, cowering before him and his sons like worshippers before an angry god.

He was so proud of those boys. They'd been waiting at the prison gate in a big fancy limousine when he'd gotten out of the slammer, and they'd taken him directly to a private mansion set up for a weekend celebration that featured willing women and good Irish whiskey. Monday morning, after their hangovers had dissipated, he'd outlined his plans and all of them had agreed with the justice of the mission. As soon as they were on board, they'd started chiming in with suggestions of their own.

Because they were their father's loyal and solid sons. Not their mother's wimps. Margaret had turned tail like the bitch she was and had deserted him when he'd been court-martialed, dishonorably discharged and sent to prison. And while he'd been rotting in that cell, she'd tried to poison the boys against him.

But he'd gotten them back and won their complete loyalty. Colin, Finn and Aidan were with him here to-night. The quartet functioned like the well-oiled commando team that he'd turned them into at their secret training camp in Washington, where he'd worked them harder than any Special Forces troops. And while he'd been doing it, he'd gotten himself back into fighting shape, too. Not that he'd let himself go to pot in prison the way some guys had done. He'd walked the prison yard and done exercises in his cell to keep fit.

But it wasn't the same as being out in the fresh air where you could take a ten-mile run. It wasn't the same as being in charge of your own life. Or working in the career where you belonged by heredity and training.

His family had served the U.S. honorably in every war since World War I. He'd expected to follow in the footsteps of his father, his uncles and his grandfather. Instead, his career had been snatched away from him by someone willing to sacrifice another man's honor to advance himself.

But tonight he and his boys would get their revenge on the men who had come out of the mission with squeaky-clean reputations.

He planned to start with Vice President Grant Davis, who'd made himself the hero of the operation. Liam had been wounded, and Davis had carried him out. Over the years, Liam had thought he might have been better off if Davis had let him bleed to death. But then, of course, he wouldn't be here now getting his revenge in spades.

Back in Georgia, Davis had used his hero status to win a hotly contested race for the Senate. After a couple of terms in the Senate, he'd been tapped to run as the vice-presidential candidate with Allan Stack and he'd used his war-hero status again to boost the prestige of the ticket.

War hero! Liam snorted, his mind spinning back to

that long-ago night in Barik. A night much like this one, with a full moon, a blackened city and a terror scenario.

For a few moments, he was back there, smelling the rank odor of a foreign city where the sewage system was hardly up to American standards, especially in the heat of a desert summer. He could hear the rockets landing and anti-aircraft units returning fire.

Even with the city under siege, it had all started off so well.

Ty Jones had ignited a minor explosion as a diversion. Then Liam was supposed to kill the power to the building, plunging it into darkness and providing cover for the coterie's entrance.

They used high-tech surveillance equipment that allowed them to see where the hostages were being held in a warren of dank basement rooms. They were ready to take out the guards in precision timing down to the nanosecond under almost impossible conditions.

Since the captors had scrambled all frequencies in the building, they were forced to rely on visual communications.

Unfortunately, Liam ended up in an alcove where he couldn't see the team leader, and *somebody* else had given him the signal to cut the power. Too soon.

With the timing off, the mission blew up in their faces. From somewhere deep in the building, one of the insurgents released cyanide gas. The team members were prepared and had masks.

But some of the innocent men and women being held hadn't made it, including Secretary of State Rollins.

Liam forced his lips into a parody of a smile.

Grant Davis had come out of the mission a hero. That wouldn't be the case tonight. Instead he'd reveal himself for the sniveling little weasel that he was. Then he'd die.

And so would the others. Ty Jones. Shane Peters, Ethan Matalon and Chase Vickers.

In the eleven years since Barik, they'd been free to do anything they wanted. Jones was a Secret Service agent. Peters had a high-class security company that catered to the rich and famous. And Matalon had a multimillion-dollar computer software company. Chase Vickers was the only underachiever of the group. A man who lacked ambition, he was content to be a limo driver. But that didn't mean he was going to escape retribution tonight.

King Frederick of Beau Pays was one of the players, too. He should have been at this reception, trapped with the other team members, but his daughter was standing in for him. When she died, it would be worse for him than if he'd taken a bullet himself.

Liam gave himself a minute to contemplate that possibility. Then he moved toward Colin.

His only regret was that Colonel Bradley, the commander of the mission, hadn't lived to get what he deserved. The colonel hadn't believed in Liam's innocence and had been one of the witnesses for the prosecution.

Well, that was all prologue. It was time to put the next phase into operation. Into the devilishly clever scenario he'd created. He'd made sure to include many details that the team members would recognize.

If they didn't get it yet, they would.

The blackout. The hostage taking. The machine

guns. The cyanide gas. The important people who would die.

Liam was prepared to die, too, if that was what it took. But his boys would get away. He'd arranged escape routes for them and new identities.

They would be safe, no matter what happened tonight.

The thought gave him a little jolt. Why was he thinking *no matter what happened?* He was totally in charge here and the night was going to come out exactly the way he intended. Unlike the last time he'd been on a mission.

Everything was running smoothly. There was no need to think about failure.

He looked over at Colin and smiled. All his boys had rallied around him, but Colin had been his chief aide in planning tonight. Colin would help him kidnap Grant Davis, while Finn and Aidan would remain behind in the tower.

OUT ON THE FLOOR, Shane reversed his direction. He'd seen, heard and smelled enough to make him sick. The men who were holding this roomful of captives were ruthless and prepared to kill as many people as they needed to accomplish their purpose.

Unfortunately, Shane couldn't be certain what that was yet.

Whatever was going down, he knew it was going to get worse. And he'd better get back to Ariana and make damn sure she didn't end up as one of the evening's casualties.

He made his way back to the crevice where he'd left Ariana. But when he reached the hiding place, he got the shock of his life.

She had disappeared.

He moved farther back into the space, hoping against hope that she'd somehow squeezed into a hidden space that he hadn't previously found. But when he reached the back wall and searched with his hands in the dark, he had to conclude that she simply wasn't there.

What the hell was she doing? What was she thinking?

Fear leaped inside him, fear fueled by anger. If he'd had her in his grasp, he would have throttled her.

But she wasn't here, and he couldn't even call out to her. Grimly, he clamped his lips together and reversed direction again. No way could she have escaped from the room. She had to be somewhere in the reception area.

He had to find her before the bad guys did.

ARIANA DRAGGED IN A DEEP breath and let it out slowly, using the technique her yoga instructor had taught her to combat stress. As the heir to the Beau Pays throne, she'd had training in what to do if she ever faced a hostage situation. But this was so totally different from anything her instructors had prepared her for.

They'd assumed she'd be the lone target at a state occasion, in a motorcade or perhaps returning to her vehicle from a public appearance, the way Ronald Reagan had been shot outside the Washington Hilton Hotel.

And they'd assumed that anyone who tried to harm her would be trying to harm the government of Beau Pays—or her father.

But this was different. She was only one of a crowd of people trapped by madmen at the top of a Boston skyscraper. Madmen who had nothing to do with her or her country.

Nobody had prepared her for this.

She stopped the train of thought before it could go any further. She was rationalizing because she was scared.

But that wasn't the fault of the security experts her father had hired to instruct her. None of them had envisioned anything like this. Neither had she. Neither had her father, or he never would have sent her here.

When the men with the guns had materialized in the middle of the reception, she'd been as shocked and scared as everyone else. She'd gone along with Peters because at the beginning of the crisis, she'd been glad to have someone big and strong protecting her.

Now that she was thinking more clearly, she knew she couldn't stay with him, hiding in a niche in the wall.

For one thing, she knew Manfred must be worried sick about her. But that wasn't the only reason for leaving the hiding place where Peters had stashed her.

She'd left her silk-and-seed pearl evening bag with Manfred when she'd decided to dance with Peters, and she had to get to it.

The purse looked like any other bag that held a woman's lipstick and comb. But inside it was a special piece of electronics equipment that she'd brought with her from home. It came from an exclusive European dealer, and her father had insisted that she take it.

It was a transmitter that would signal she was in trouble. But it also included a broadcast function that would send out voice transmissions. Not just voices, but the sound of gunfire as well.

She wanted the world to know what was going on in this reception room. Maybe it was their only link to the outside world, since the men who held the guests captive had taken away all the cell phones and walkie-talkies. She still had her covert device, but it was inactive at the moment. She needed to get to it so she could turn it on.

Of course, she hadn't heard anything from the president or the vice president since the crisis had begun, and maybe in the dark and confusion, the Secret Service had gotten them out of the building and had sent help on the way. But she couldn't count on it. Her father had taught her that in a crisis, you must rely on yourself.

She'd had martial-arts instruction and weapons training. Though, like Peters, she hadn't been able to bring a gun to this reception. Above and beyond her training, she was in excellent physical shape. Plus, she was wearing a valuable ring and necklace that she was authorized to exchange for her freedom. But it seemed that these men weren't interested in riches, or they would have already started stripping the guests of their jewels.

She grimaced. So far, she hadn't done much for herself in this crisis. Or for the Beau Pays sapphire, either. Was it safe? She hoped so, but she had a more urgent problem now. She'd blindly followed Shane Peters into hiding. Now she had to get to that transmitter and turn it on.

She'd seen Peters crawl out of their hiding place and use a linen-covered table to shield himself from view. Now she did the same.

Before she'd left home, she'd been given background information on the building and the reception area, but, in a rush to leave, she'd only given the sheets a quick scan. Leaning back against the wall, she closed her eyes and tried to bring up a picture of the room, searching mentally for another way out besides the main entrance.

There had to be stairs. And a service entrance used by caterers.

The gunmen had been blocking that door. Were they still there?

Long ago, she and her brother had played hide-and-seek in the palace, crawling around the heavily carved furniture and richly upholstered couches and chairs, and leaping out to scare each other. For just a moment she let herself think about those simpler days when life hadn't been so full of responsibilities.

Rolf had been her father's hope for the future, but when he had died, that hope had come down squarely on her own shoulders.

Stop thinking about any of that, she ordered herself. *You're in the middle of a crisis, and you have to get yourself out of it.*

With her lower lip between her teeth, she started crawling in back of the tables, keeping out of sight of the men with the guns and masks.

She'd compared this to her childhood adventures. But when she'd crawled around on the floor long ago, she'd been wearing casual clothing—not an expensive evening gown. Her knees slid against the stiff Thai silk, and she was forced to stop and pull the skirt up around her hips, balling up the excess fabric in the crook of her arm as she worked her way toward where she'd last seen Manfred and her evening bag.

FINN SHEA LOOKED AROUND with satisfaction at the well-dressed crowd of men and women cowering in the center of the room like shell-shocked refugees who had been directed to a bomb shelter to wait out a terrorist attack. Only the attack was right here in the room, not somewhere outside.

His father had been right. It had taken only a few killings to get them under control. The first deaths had been random, to show these people who was boss.

Soon they would get down to the real business of the evening. But first he was going to collect an extra little dividend.

"I'll be right back."

"Make it quick," his father said.

Leaving his father and his brothers to keep the crowd under control, he walked to the far side of the room, to the case where the ridiculously gaudy Beau Pays sapphire was on display.

The security system was electronic, and with the power off there was nothing to stop anyone from taking the jewel. Too bad for King Frederick. Finn knew the old man would be devastated when he found out the family treasure was missing. That was only going to add to the misery of losing his daughter.

Through the lenses of Finn's night-vision goggles, the sapphire glowed a strange shade of green.

But he knew the true color, because he had studied many pictures of the gem.

Quickly he extracted the metal tool he'd brought along for the purpose, then used it to break the lock on the thick Lucite case.

It opened as smoothly as a can of sardines, and he pulled out the sapphire.

But the moment he held the gem in his hand, he knew something was wrong. He'd studied all the physical specifications of the sapphire, and he knew the weight of the faceted stone. This thing was far too light.

He hefted it in his hand, then for another check, he scraped it across the Lucite. The gem didn't even make a scratch. The damn thing that had been in this case all evening wasn't the Beau Pays sapphire. It was a fake.

He muttered a curse, then ordered himself to think through the situation.

Had the counterfeit really been in the case since the beginning of the reception?

When he'd first arrived and begun his waiter duties, he'd taken a look at the gem. No question it had been the real thing. Now it was missing.

And he had a good idea where it had gone. Just before the president had arrived, Shane Peters had been hanging around the case.

Finn cursed under his breath as he worked out what must have happened. Peters was known as a daredevil. And he owned a security company that catered to the rich and famous. What if he'd wanted to get King Frederick for a client? He could have just applied for the job like any normal human being. Made a proposal for how he'd do things differently.

But that was too easy for a hotshot like Peters. Finn had a hunch that the man had set out to demonstrate his superior technology tonight by playing a little trick on the king.

Well, that wouldn't do Mr. Smart-Ass Peters a lot of good. Because he wasn't getting out of this building alive. Not tonight.

One of their first priorities would be to find him and make him tell where he'd hidden the gem. Or maybe he was carrying it around?

A ninety-carat sapphire? Unlikely. But it would be gratifying to make Peters tell what he'd done with it.

Finn had read up on the career of the great Shane Peters. At least what was on the public record. There was probably a lot more, if you had the right government sources and maybe sources that weren't prepared to go on record.

He'd seen enough to know that Peters had done the same thing in his career as Grant Davis. Had used his army experience to establish his civilian credentials, although in a different venue.

Peters acted as if he were hot stuff, which would make it all the sweeter when he started squealing like a stuck pig begging for his life.

Finn made a split-second decision. He would tell his brothers that Peters had taken the sapphire, so they could be on the lookout for the gem. But he would protect Dad from the annoying information.

His father had planned every detail of this evening, and Finn wanted to see his scenario play out as the old man had envisioned it. There was no point in telling him that something had briefly gone a little bit off track— not when they could get it to work out the way it was supposed to. And Dad would never be the wiser.

Chapter Five

Ariana silently railed against her long skirt as she kept crawling across the floor, using the tables as a shield.

She had made it partway around the room when the man who was running the horror show began speaking again. She went rigid as his voice boomed out across the reception room.

She could tell he was enjoying this situation, and she wanted to slap him across his smug face. Of course, that would only get her killed, so she clenched her teeth and waited.

"All right, you bunch of self-satisfied capitalists. I want the president and the vice president. I know their Secret Service guards have hidden them away in some nook up here, but they can't escape. So hand them over."

There were murmurs around the room. One man shouted, "You have to be kidding."

A woman started to moan, and others in the group tried to hush her.

Ariana risked a peek from around the table where she was hiding. She could see the men with the guns, see their relaxed posture. They were the kings of this little terrorist state that they had created. One of them leaned over to speak to another, and the second one laughed softly.

The laugh made her want to throw up.

She knew in that moment that they weren't staging this hostage situation out of grim necessity. They were like men who had gone out on one of those hunting farms to shoot game that someone had raised for the purpose. They were perfectly comfortable with killing to get what they wanted. And they had obviously practiced their moves and knew how to make the evening work to their advantage.

As if to confirm her assessment, their leader gave another clipped demand to the people at his mercy.

"I want the president and vice president immediately. If you don't turn them over, then I will begin shooting a hostage every ten minutes." He paused to let that sink in, waiting until the moans and protests had subsided. Then he added another horrifying detail. "And the first person we kill will be Princess Ariana of Beau Pays."

Ariana's blood turned cold. These men knew she was here. They were looking for her, and they were going to kill her first.

So what would happen if one of the other captives saw her?

From childhood, she'd been trained to understand people and their motivations. There were always good and bad individuals in every crowd. Some of these terrified partygoers would turn her in to curry favor with the enemy.

And others would risk their lives to save her, like the people who had risked execution to hide Jews from the Nazis.

But whatever the other people in this room did, she

knew she had made a strategic mistake. She should have stayed in the hiding place Peters had found.

Did she have a chance of getting back there?

Her horror increased as she saw one of the killers plunge into the crowd and pull a man up to the front of the room.

When she saw it was Manfred, her heart leaped into her throat. He had sworn to protect her with his life, and she knew he would do it.

"This is the princess's bodyguard," the kidnapper said to his companions.

"Oh yeah?" one of them answered, then turned to Manfred. "Where is she?"

"I don't know. Maybe she left."

Absolute silence had fallen over the crowd as they watched the unfolding drama.

The kidnapper raised his gun and slammed it against Manfred's cheek. "Don't lie to me!"

Ariana crammed her fist against her mouth to keep from crying out.

Manfred gasped but kept his rigid stance. "If I knew where she was, I wouldn't tell you."

"You have three seconds to answer," the man with the gun said, his voice hard. "Or I'm going to kill you instead of her."

"Go to hell," Manfred answered, his own voice steady. He'd always been so cool and collected, and that had gotten him nowhere in this situation.

She knew Manfred had been in love with her for a long time. It was a hopeless love that he could never fulfill. She'd told her father about it and asked for another guard. Her father had answered that the situation made Manfred more willing to sacrifice himself for her.

As she watched in horror, he turned and leaped at the lead thug, taking the man completely by surprise. Manfred would have knocked him to the ground if he hadn't been standing so close to the wall.

Still on his feet, the man struggled with Manfred. One of the other gunmen turned and began firing.

People screamed and backed away as Manfred went down and lay unmoving on the floor.

For a moment, chaos reigned in the room, and Ariana thought that the gunman might have lost control of the situation. If all these people rushed their captors, some would be killed. But they would ultimately take the bad guys out.

But this group of captives wasn't the equal of the passengers on flight ninety-three who had forced their hijacked plane down in a Pennsylvania field. They were too frightened to risk their lives.

When one of the gunmen bellowed, "Settle down, or you'll all get what he got," the crowd quieted as though someone had stuffed gags in their mouths.

"Too bad the princess's bodyguard can't tell us where she is," the speaker announced coolly. "But she can't escape from this room, and we'll find her."

Ariana bit down on her knuckles, welcoming the sudden pain. There was nothing she could do for Manfred. Nothing except weep. And she couldn't even allow herself that outlet for her grief because crying would give her away.

Manfred was dead, but she had to stay alive. For her father. For her country. And for another reason, too. These men had said she was next. If they couldn't find her, that might save the lives of the others in the room.

At least for a while. If they couldn't find her, they

might start on some of the other guests. Then she'd have a horrible moral dilemma. She'd have to turn herself in or watch more people die in her place.

But for the time being, she was going to stay hidden.

As quietly and as quickly as she could, she started retracing her route to the wall slot, moving backward on her hands and knees.

Before she'd crawled two feet, a hand grabbed her from behind. She started to scream, but her captor pressed his palm firmly over her mouth.

Desperately she tried to twist away, but he held her in his iron grip.

IN A LOCKED STRONGHOLD at the side of the room, President Allan Stack and Vice President Grant Davis listened to the words of the gunman.

President Stack made an angry sound. "It sounds like this operation has been planned down to the last detail."

Davis nodded. In the light from the flashlights the Secret Service agents were holding, the vice president looked gray and sick. Stack imagined that he didn't look much better, but he did know his moral obligation.

Two agents were with them. Trusted men. They'd gotten them into a service area with a sturdy door. But now what?

"What do we do?" Davis asked his personal agent, Ty Jones.

Stack answered before Jones could give an opinion. "I think we have to surrender, or people will die."

"We can't," Davis objected.

"Do you have a better plan?" the president asked.

"Send in a rescue team."

Stack looked at Charlie Mercer, the agent in charge of his safety. "Is that feasible?"

"It would be possible," the agent answered, his tone making it clear that the strategy was risky.

"But before they could pull us out of here, a lot of people would die when the hostage takers start shooting," Stack said.

"Yes, sir."

"Do we know who they are?"

Mercer shook his head. "We don't know who they are, and we don't know their motivation."

A shadow flickered across Davis's face.

"Do you have some information?" Stack demanded.

"No, sir." He cleared his throat. "I say we wait for a rescue operation."

"I don't think so," Stack answered. "They said they'd already shot three people. And we just heard more gunfire."

"Can we give it a few minutes?" Davis asked.

"Eight minutes," Stack answered. "And if I hear more shots out there, we open the door."

THE CAPTOR WHO HELD ARIANA in viselike arms shifted his grip so he could bring his lips to her ear. When he spoke, she had trouble making sense of the words at first. Then they penetrated her paralyzed brain.

"It's Shane Peters. I'll take my hand away if you don't scream."

She nodded, then sagged in his arms as he turned her and held her to him.

She wanted to cling to him. She wanted to thank God that he'd found her.

Again his mouth came up against her ear. "What the hell are you doing?"

Nobody had ever spoken to her like that, and she stiffened. But from his point of view, she understood that he thought he had the right to be angry with her.

She turned so that she could whisper in his ear. "There's a signal device combined with a transmitter in my evening bag. I was trying to turn it on."

"Too dangerous," he answered.

"I'll be the judge of that."

"I think you have to trust my judgment for the moment, since I'm the security expert."

Logic told her he was right. He was the trained operative, and she was only the princess in distress. Even if she didn't like his methods at the moment, she knew he was trying to save her life.

Just as he started to lead her back the way they'd come, she heard footsteps on the wooden floor coming straight toward them.

When she froze, Peters looked around, then quickly pushed her under the round table closest to them. As he crawled in after her, he pulled the linen cloth down behind him.

The metal legs took up a lot of the floor space underneath, so they had to curl their bodies around each other to fit. There was no room to move, no room to do more than cling to each other.

She pressed her cheek against Shane's shoulder. Now that she was thinking a little more clearly, she realized that he could have returned to their hiding place any time he'd wanted. But he had chosen to come looking for her.

As the footsteps came close, she clutched his hand, meshing her fingers with his, drawing strength from him because she had almost run out of her own resources. As they huddled together under the table, she understood that she had misjudged him at first, because she had never known anyone like him.

There were men her age in her country who had strength of character. Men who were wise. Men who had physical prowess and daring. But Shane Peters seemed to embody a unique mix of all of these characteristics.

He held her absolutely still, but she felt the tension in his body. If the man stopped beside their table, if he lifted the cloth, Peters was prepared to spring out at him.

She closed her eyes, wishing she could pretend she was somewhere else and this was some other time.

What if she and Shane had taken the brazen step of slipping away earlier in the evening? Or what if she were on a longer trip to the United States and she'd met him at a party at a mansion outside Washington, D.C.?

Yes, that was a lot better than reality.

They'd danced and talked and wandered out into the garden where they could be alone, and Manfred had stayed at a respectful distance. The thought of her bodyguard sent a stab of pain through her, and she instantly turned her focus back to Shane.

What if they'd wandered down a garden path and found a charming little guesthouse with a romantic bedroom? They'd stepped inside and closed the door, and now they were alone together on a wide mattress, where they were lying close.

She let her mind take her further into the dreamworld that was so much safer, so much more appealing than the reality of this horror show.

She pressed her cheek against Shane's, and he

returned the pressure. They were still dressed, but he'd do something about that soon. He'd shrug out of his tuxedo jacket, then he'd work the zipper at the back of her dress. Or maybe he'd wait on that awhile.

She imagined herself playing with the stiff fabric of his dress shirt. Then she'd begin opening the studs down the front so that she could explore his wide chest with her fingers.

Was his chest smooth? Or did he have dark hair that matched the hair on his head?

As she wrapped herself in the tempting fantasy, her breath quickened.

Shane turned his head, and she knew his gaze was on her, even if she couldn't see him in their dark cave. Because she was responding to him, she felt her cheeks heat and was glad he couldn't see the flush, even if he could feel it.

She had created the fantasy, yet he seemed to be reading her mind. He turned his face so that he could press his lips to her cheek, then slide them slowly, tantalizingly to her mouth.

His touch was light and tender. Like a lover who knew his partner was far less experienced in bed than he was and needed him to go slowly.

Had he guessed that, too? Did he know that the daughter of King Frederick of Beau Pays had very little knowledge of man-woman intimacy?

She hardly knew Shane Peters, yet he reached her in ways no other man had managed before. When he brushed his mouth back and forth against hers, she drew in a quick, shaky breath, entranced by the softness of his lips. She'd admired their shape; now she loved their texture.

In the darkness, she felt him smile, heard him make a small, urgent sound. The tip of his tongue stroked against the seam of her lips, and she opened for him, allowing him an intimacy that few others had ever dared request.

He stroked the sensitive tissue just inside her lips, then swept along the line of her teeth before delving a little deeper, tasting her, sipping from her, sending heat through her body.

Somewhere in the back of her mind, she was amazed at her own behavior as she gave herself over to the hot arousal he was kindling within her. She found herself craving more of what he could give her.

He shifted a little, moving his mouth away from hers, and she felt disappointment knife through her. But he had only slid his lips back along her cheek, then to her earlobe, where he paused to nibble with the strong white teeth that had earlier flashed at her in a sexy grin.

Then his tongue traced the curve of her ear, stiffened and probed inside, and she shivered with awareness, surprised that the touch of tongue to ear could be so erotic.

She hadn't known. But then, there was so much she didn't know about arousing a partner.

His hand moved to the column of her neck, stroking up and down, then playing with her collarbone. When her breath quickened, he let his hand drift lower, to the top of her breast where it swelled above the bodice of her gown.

He stroked her skin there, sending hot currents shooting through her body.

She imagined his hand drifting lower, slipping inside

her dress so that he could cup the fullness of her breast, pressing against her beaded nipple.

She wanted him to touch her there, wanted him to ease the ache that he'd kindled inside her.

But the footsteps outside their refuge intruded rudely on the fantasy, and she jerked back, as though she'd been caught listening outside the grand council chamber in the palace.

At the moment, she wasn't a girl listening outside her father's door and feeling the delicious thrill of hearing what she thought were state secrets. She was a hostage in a very dangerous situation, and her mind abruptly re-engaged with reality.

As she tried to picture the floor outside the table, she remembered her long gown and had to stop herself from gathering the skirt closer around her legs. If she moved a muscle, the stiff Thai silk would rustle and surely give them both away.

But what if a piece of her skirt was sticking out? It would be like the Beau Pays flag lying on the floor.

The footsteps stopped, and she felt Shane prepare for action.

Mon Dieu. She'd tried to put Manfred out of her mind. Now she was afraid Shane was going to get killed, too, and she couldn't stand it.

When she started to move, Shane grabbed her arm, his fingers digging into her flesh, the same fingers that had been so sweetly sensual just a few moments earlier. The harsh grip centered her, and she understood how close she'd come to getting them both shot.

Just then, the man in charge of the whole nightmare started to speak again. "Ladies and gentlemen, I'm losing patience. Someone in this room knows where to find Princess Ariana LeBron. You have five minutes to turn her over to us, or I'm going to start the executions with someone else."

Chapter Six

Ariana went cold all over, expecting the man standing beside the table to reach down, sweep aside the table-cloth and jerk her to her feet. When he had her in his iron grip, he would lead her triumphantly through the crowd to the place of execution.

Instead, he moved rapidly back toward the front of the room, and she let out a small, shaky breath.

In the middle of the room, a woman began to sob. A man cursed. And Peters gathered Ariana closer.

"You're doing great," he whispered.

"Hardly."

His arms were like a safe haven, and she wanted to stay wrapped in his warmth. But she couldn't allow herself to do that. Not after what she'd just heard. "You have to let me go," she said in a defeated voice.

His grip on her tightened, and she knew he could hold her here against her will if he wanted to.

"Are you crazy?" he snapped. "If you go out there, you're committing suicide."

She could barely speak, but she managed to get the words out. "They're going to kill innocent people because of me. I can't let that happen."

"That's not your fault."

"But I can't live with it."

THE DEADLY ANNOUNCEMENT also penetrated the service closet where President Allan Stack, Vice President Davis and the two Secret Service men were hiding.

Allan turned to his vice president. "That settles it. We have to go out there."

Charlie Mercer, the Secret Service agent in charge, weighed in immediately with the line Allan had expected him to deliver. "I wouldn't advise that, sir."

Allan turned toward the man. They'd been in some tough spots together. Like the time in Sào Paulo when a hostile crowd had surrounded their car and started pelting them with rocks. They'd managed to drive out of that crisis. But they weren't in a bulletproof car now.

"I know you wouldn't advise me to turn myself in," he said softly to the man who was sworn to protect him with his life. "You got me in here because it's safe, and it seemed like a good idea at the time. We both thought someone would be able to rescue us before things got hairy. But it hasn't happened. And if we stay in this closet, innocent people will die."

"But, sir—"

Allan waved the agent to silence. "We'll only be postponing the inevitable. Sooner or later, the armed men out there will get through this door. If they have to shoot their way in, they'll kill us."

"If we go out there, we could be killed anyway," Davis muttered, then turned to Ty Jones, the agent who headed his Secret Service detail.

"I agree with Mercer," Jones answered immediately.

Allan gave the young man a steady look. "Of course

you agree with Mercer. That's your training speaking. But I think if we go out, we have a reasonable chance of survival. The bad guys went to a lot of trouble to set this up. If they'd wanted to kill us, they could have done it as soon as the lights went out."

Jones answered with a tight nod.

"How are you going to feel if they start shooting innocent people?" Allan asked Grant Davis.

"Horrible." He cleared his throat. "But they have cyanide gas."

"Is that worse than machine guns?"

Davis looked as if he still wanted to argue, but he firmed his jaw and straightened his shoulders, because any further protests would brand him as a coward. Allan was sure that the last thing Davis wanted to do was tarnish his image as a war hero.

Allan had picked him partly for his ability to pull in the military vote, since he himself had never been in the armed forces. Almost immediately after the election, however, he'd started regretting his choice. But he was stuck with Davis, until the next election. If they made it to the next election. He was talking a good game in here, but he didn't really know if they'd come out of this alive.

"Go ahead and tell them we're coming out," Davis said, his voice edged with raw nerves.

"Thank you," Allan whispered.

WHEN ARIANA STARTED to struggle with Shane, he closed his fingers over her shoulder, holding her in place.

"No," he growled, then wondered if his harsh word would bring the madmen with the machine guns charging over.

He waited for heart-stopping seconds, wishing he had a weapon more substantial than his damn plastic knife.

So how had the guys out there managed to get guns up here? Bribery? Apparently they'd planned this mission down to the tiniest details.

But Ariana was screwing up their plans by evading them. That must be making them crazy.

She started to speak, then stopped abruptly as an unexpected voice cut through the darkness.

"This is Allan Stack, president of the United States. We're willing to surrender if you guarantee the safety of the people in this room."

"That's not acceptable. I guarantee nothing," the leader of the assailants shouted back.

"Then why should we surrender?"

"Because if you don't, I'll kill innocent people. Is that what you and Grant Davis want?"

The way he said Davis's name sent a shudder down Shane's spine. The man in charge of this horror show had maintained a civil tone with the president until he'd mentioned Grant Davis. The man who had been on the rescue mission in Barik. Further confirmation, in Shane's mind, that tonight's blackout and hostage situation went back to that specific episode.

Shane glanced toward Ariana. He couldn't see her in the dark under the tablecloth, but he knew she waited tensely for the outcome of the verbal exchange. Knew that what happened in the next few minutes would dictate her fate.

As a patriotic American, it sickened him to think about President Stack and Vice President Davis surrendering to armed hostage takers. It was always the policy of the United States never to negotiate with terrorists. That was fine in the abstract. But in this situation, negotiating sounded like the best alternative.

He poked his head out from under the table and saw shadowy outlines of people, visible only because of the moonlight coming through the windows. Then he blinked as a brighter light burst through the darkness.

It came from a high-powered flashlight.

"Put that damn light out!" the ringleader shouted.

"Take off your night-vision goggles," a sharp voice countered. He recognized it as Ty Jones.

"I believe we're the ones in charge here. Put out the light if you don't want to get shot."

After several seconds, the light snapped out.

"Nobody move," one of their captors shouted. "Except Stack, Davis and their Secret Service agents."

The crowd of men and women in the center of the room had been given a direct order. They stayed where they were, but an undercurrent of voices rose up in their midst. Probably most of them were expressing their relief, Shane thought.

"Quiet!" the leader of the madmen bellowed. To reinforce his words, he shot at random into the crowd.

Screams of pain and terror erupted.

Beside Shane, Ariana made a strangled sound as bullets hit the floor only inches from their hiding place.

"We're getting out of here," Shane whispered, knitting his fingers with hers. "Stay low." He'd led her to one hiding place already. He hoped that in the confusion he could get her out of the room.

TY JONES'S HEART WAS POUNDING, but he maintained an icy outward calm as three of the armed men hustled him, the president, Vice President Davis and Agent Mercer into the kitchen. Emergency lights illuminated the area, and the gunmen took off their night-vision goggles but not their gas masks. To hide their identities or because they were going to open the canisters of cyanide gas?

Ty tried to get a look at their faces, but the masks made it difficult to see their features. Well, at least he could report their hair color, height and probable weight.

One of them rudely shoved the vice president, who almost lost his footing, but Ty kept his lips pressed together. These men had already proved they were wildly unpredictable. Challenging them could be fatal.

"Stack and Davis, over there," one of the gunmen barked.

The president and vice president moved to the side of the room, where one of the men kept his gun trained on them.

First they searched Ty and Mercer for communications equipment, then pushed them into chairs that were waiting for them.

As Ty watched helplessly, they threw cell phones, transmitters and receivers onto the floor and crushed them under their heels.

"Hands behind your backs."

They did as they were told. One of the captors held them all at gunpoint while the other used rope and duct tape to secure Mercer to the chair.

Ty thought about making a move before they got to him, but he knew he would only be committing suicide. And maybe he'd take the president and vice president with him.

So he gritted his teeth and waited while one of the bastards secured his hands and feet to the chair. Next, they gagged both him and Mercer with the duct tape, then turned their chairs so they couldn't see each other.

The last sight he had of President Stack and Vice President Davis was of two gunmen hustling them out the door. The other returned to the reception room.

As soon as they were gone, Ty started working on his bonds. They were tight, but as he looked around in the dim emergency lighting, he saw a metal edge on one of the kitchen drawers. Maybe he could use it to cut the rope.

Awkwardly he maneuvered his chair across the floor. Each time the chair moved an inch, it thumped on the kitchen tile and he stopped, waiting with his heart pounding to see if he'd drawn the attention of the thugs in the reception area. When nobody came through the door, he thumped again and waited. It took fifteen agonizing minutes, but finally he reached the drawer and began sawing with his wrists against the metal corner.

He worked feverishly, aware that his escape attempt could get him killed. If one of the other gunmen came back here and found Ty sawing at his bonds, he'd probably get shot in the head.

That was only one of the ugly thoughts racing through his mind.

He had been so elated when he'd gotten the assignment of guarding the vice president. He'd been on this detail less than a year, and now he had lost the man in his care. In the Secret Service, no agent's career survived a stain like that.

But his first thought wasn't just about his own future. It was about Grant Davis.

He and the vice president went way back. They'd both been in the Special Forces, and they'd met when they'd started training for that rescue mission in Barik. He'd admired Davis's grace under fire back then. And he still admired the man. He was proud to say that they were friends—or as close as possible when one was a highly placed public official and the other was his bodyguard.

They had gotten to know and respect each other on that long-ago operation. They'd both gone on to other assignments and lost touch over the years, but when Davis had been elected vice president, he'd specifically asked for Ty as the agent in charge of his protection. That was quite an honor, and until this hellish night, Ty had done the job well.

Now he was feeling sick as he looked at the door behind which the president and vice president had disappeared with their kidnappers.

What the hell was the other agent doing? Ty wished he knew.

But his best alternative was to worry about himself. He had to get free, to send a message to the detail outside, telling them that the president and vice president were on their way down—with two crazed gunmen.

SHANE GRABBED ARIANA'S HAND and tugged. "Come on."

"Where?"

"Out of here."

"They're not going to kill me now."

"You don't know that. You don't have any idea what these guys are going to do for their next big move. They can open fire on the room again, and there's no point in your trying for martyr status."

To his vast relief, she was still thinking rationally enough to let him lead her away from the action. Now he had to hope that the bad guys were still at the front of the room, and not at the main entrance where the guests had come in.

CHASE VICKERS SAT IN THE limo, his six-foot-one frame hunched in the driver's seat as he sat in traffic. He banged the steering wheel in frustration. It wasn't only the miles of cars in front of him. He'd been on edge all night, ever since the lights had gone out all over Boston. Now he felt like jumping out of his skin.

But he wasn't an ordinary driver. He had a security clearance to escort foreign dignitaries and government officials all over the United States and abroad. Another man might have made that his main career. He used it as a way of filling his time when he wasn't on an Eclipse assignment.

He lived for those assignments. They were the only time he really felt alive.

And he wanted to get into action now.

Unable to sit still, he absently rubbed the scar again. He'd gotten it during a mercenary mission in Afghanistan, and sometimes when he was under stress it throbbed.

It was pulsing like a son of a bitch now.

Taking a deep breath, he forced himself to settle down. No use acting like a mongoose in a cage. Right now the only thing he could do was sit and wait.

UPSTAIRS, SHANE STAYED on his hands and knees, moving Ariana steadily toward the west end of the room, toward the entrance where they'd first come in. The elevators were located in the foyer, but so was an exit door that led to a corridor that intersected the back stairs.

If they could slip through the doorway, they could escape. But was that the right thing to do? Their captor had said that if they tried to leave, they'd trigger the release of cyanide gas. Yet all through the nightmare captivity, Shane had been thinking about the psychology of Liam Shea, trying to figure out what mind games the bastard was playing.

If it was Liam Shea running the show. Shane had been betting that it was, and he'd come to the conclusion that Liam Shea had thrown in the canister of gas as an effective means of crowd control.

His other reason was more complicated. Liam had set this evening up to match the long-ago raid in Barik. That night there had been darkness, hostages, machine guns and cyanide gas.

Shane was thinking that tonight it didn't really exist.

He was willing to bet his life on his logic. But could he risk Ariana's life?

Chapter Seven

"What's wrong?" Ariana whispered.

Shane peered through the doorway. It was absolutely dark inside the foyer, except for the tantalizing red exit sign thirty feet away, which must have been operating on battery power. The exit spelled freedom from this nightmare. Yet it might as well have been on the other side of the earth for all the good it did him.

"They said there was cyanide gas at the exits," he whispered.

"Not at this entrance," she said, sounding very positive about her information.

He turned to her in the darkness. "How do you know?"

"Because just as I was arriving, the Secret Service was sweeping this area. If there had been a canister of gas, they would have found it."

"They could have placed it later," he argued.

"How could they? I came in with a crowd of people, and more guests were coming in the whole time. They couldn't set up a trap like that in full view of everybody, could they?"

He thought about that logic. Her theory made sense, yet he was still reluctant to risk her life.

While he was trying to decide what to do, Ariana crawled across the threshold.

He muffled a gasp, then charged across after her, still on his hands and knees.

It was several seconds before he realized that nothing had happened. They were still breathing the building's stale air.

Not cyanide.

And no men with gas masks were running after them shooting. A very good sign. They both crawled to the side of the entrance hall, out of sight from the main room. Ariana sat, leaning against the wall, breathing hard.

"Dieu merci," she whispered.

"We're not safe yet."

He reached for her hand and helped her up, then led her along the wall, toward the exit light. And he didn't give thanks until he grasped the cold metal of the doorknob and found that it really did turn in his hand.

He eased the door open and ushered Ariana into the corridor. Like the exit sign, it was glowing with low-level emergency lighting.

Closing the door behind them, he made a rough sound. Then, because he needed to express his thanks in a very physical way, he pulled Ariana into his arms and crushed her against his chest.

He had held her before. On the dance floor, in the crevice where they'd hidden and under the table, where they'd huddled together and he had kissed her.

That had been a sweet kiss. A kiss born of anguish. He had wanted her to know how much she had come to mean to him and so quickly. At the same time, he had been desperate to keep her away from those gunmen, and he had used the sexual pull between them to draw her in and keep her safe from harm.

But now that they had escaped from the killing field, his relief swelled over into action.

With no thought that she would reject him, he dipped his head toward her mouth, his lips sealing to hers, his mouth rapacious as he devoured her.

She could have pulled back. But she met him more than halfway, and he knew that her emotions had leaped up to meet his.

He had made love to many women. Lusty, satisfying love. But as his hands slid down Ariana's back, molding her body to his, he felt a wave of need stronger than anything he had ever experienced in his lifetime.

The kiss was fueled by relief and greed. His and hers.

He drew her lower lip into his mouth, sucking, nibbling, overwhelmed by the small sounds of arousal that she made.

He was dressed in a tuxedo and she was wearing a stiff silk evening dress. Yet the image in his head was of the two of them naked, holding each other, rocking together on a wide bed.

She moaned into his mouth. As he drank in the sound, he stroked his fingers across her bare back, then slipped them under the top of her dress, dipping inside the fabric for more intimate contact, entranced by the warm skin of her back.

She moaned again as he cupped her bottom and lifted her up, pulling her against his erection.

His blood was on fire. He wanted her with a force

that was close to madness. All thought had left his mind—except the need to merge his body with hers.

She gasped at the contact, clung to his broad shoulders as the white-hot kiss drugged his senses.

Amazingly, the world had vanished, leaving only the two of them. He rocked her in his arms, loving the friction against his supercharged body. Blindly, his fingers fumbled at the back of her gown. Finding the tab of her zipper, he felt as though he'd been given the key to a priceless treasure. He'd have her naked soon, her body under his.

But as he began to lower the zipper, Ariana stiffened in his arms.

He lifted his head, blinking in the dim light. He had forgotten where they were. Forgotten everything besides the woman in his arms.

Firmly, she pushed against his shoulder. "Shane, please. Don't. We can't."

"Why not?"

"I can't…" she repeated, her voice breaking as she said the words.

It took a moment for him to realize what she was saying, to realize why she was pushing him away.

He swallowed, struggling to bring himself under control. He'd gone a little crazy with wanting her. He understood that truth on a gut-wrenching level. Nothing like this had ever happened to him in his life. Sex was a fun activity where he and his partner gave each other pleasure. It had never been a wild ride where need took over for rational thought.

Until now.

"I'm sorry," he managed to say, hearing the thickness in his voice.

She kept her gaze steady, though he was sure she wanted to look away. "It was as much my fault as yours," she murmured. "But…I can't."

"I understand that," he answered. "And I also know that I shouldn't have started anything."

She answered with a tight nod, and he knew that he had to keep his hands off her. She might have been swept along by the passion of the moment, but she wasn't a woman who could indulge in casual affairs.

The assessment brought him up short.

Casual? Not hardly.

They might have just met tonight, but what they'd been doing together hadn't felt like a one-night stand. Which was all the more reason he had to follow a hands-off policy.

Now that his head was more or less screwed on straight, he'd better think about what he was supposed to be doing—getting her out of this tower of terror.

Once again he wished to hell he had a gun. Instead, he had to settle for the fire extinguisher on the wall. He lifted it off the metal brace, thinking that he could use it as a club. It would be good as a spray, too, if only the bad guys weren't wearing gas masks.

The masks were only for effect, he reminded himself, since there wasn't any cyanide gas. At least at the main entrance to the reception area.

Too bad there was no way to get the information about the gas to the people remaining in the room.

"We have to get downstairs," he said, hearing the gritty quality of his own voice.

She looked around the hallway. "How?"

"There are stairs around the corner."

"How do you know?"

"I'm always thorough. I studied the layout of the building before the party."

He was glad she didn't ask why he'd needed the information. He sure as hell wasn't going to tell her that it was part of his plan to steal her country's famous sapphire. Or that he had the damn thing in the hidden pocket inside his tuxedo sleeve.

They reached the end of the hall, and he stopped, motioning for her to wait. In the dim glow of the emergency lighting, he looked around the corner. The hallway was clear, and the door to the stairs was only a few feet away.

Was it safe to risk a call?

He pulled out his cell phone and punched in one of the auto-dial numbers. But a computerized voice told him the circuits were busy.

"Who were you trying to call?" Ariana asked at his side.

"My brother."

She nodded, trying to take that in. "He's on site?"

"He's a limo driver and he has a special clearance to drive dignitaries. I thought maybe he was outside."

"Oh," was all she could manage.

She hadn't known Shane Peters had a brother. She remembered that Shane was a millionaire. And he had a brother who was a limo driver? That seemed rather strange. But why not? Everything tonight was strange.

The hostage taking. The kidnapping. The deaths.

She pulled her mind away from the deaths, from Manfred's especially. She knew she could still join her bodyguard.

She would have liked to just shut her mind down and follow Shane Peters out of here. But she couldn't stop the terrible images from whirling in her head.

To keep her thoughts away from death and destruction, she focused on the way she'd behaved with Shane. She had ended up in his arms. And if they'd been in a bedroom, she would have let him take off her dress. And more.

Unbelievable, considering that duty to her country had been drummed into her since she was a little girl. One thing she had always known, she had to be a virgin when she married.

So was she the only twenty-nine-year-old virgin left in the world? She repressed a hysterical laugh. Maintaining that status hadn't been so difficult until she'd met Shane Peters. Then suddenly, all the rules that had been drummed into her flew out of her head.

Well, she'd better remember them. And she'd better remember that she and this man could never be more to each other than casual friends.

In her real life, it took her a long time to get to know anyone on more than a superficial level. She'd cut through her usual reserve pretty quickly with Shane. But the danger of the hostage situation had created an atmosphere of intimacy between them that would never have existed otherwise.

Even as that rationalization surfaced, she knew she was kidding herself. It had started before the armed men had taken over the reception, when she'd first seen the devastatingly handsome man across the room. Then she'd danced with him and melted into his arms.

She was so caught up in her thoughts that she didn't realize they'd reached the door to the stairs. Shane looked back at her and put his fingers to his lips, and she knew he was worried about what might be on the other side of this door.

He moved her back a few yards, then pulled the door open with one hand, the fire extinguisher raised in the other.

When he saw the stairwell was empty, he ushered her through. Because she still had on her high heels, it was hard to walk quickly. So she pulled them off and held them by the sling backs in her left hand, gripping the railing with her right.

They had descended two floors when he stopped short again.

Looking around his large frame, she saw what had stopped his downward progress.

A man wearing a tuxedo lay sprawled across the steps—either dead or unconscious.

One of the gunmen or one of the guests? And was he only playing dead? If they came close, would he spring up and grab them?

Ariana allowed Shane to keep his body between her and the crumpled figure as he descended the stairs. Kneeling down, he put his hand on the man's shoulder, then quickly rolled him over.

Mon Dieu.

Ariana gasped when she saw the man's face.

It was President Allan Stack, his skin gray and pasty and his lips pale.

Not far from him on the floor was a pool of blood.

"Is he dead?" Ariana gasped out as she focused on the red spill.

"I don't know." Shane crouched on one side of the leader of the free world. He felt for a pulse in the man's neck, then leaned over to feel his breath against his cheek.

"He's alive."

"Dieu merci."

Swiftly Shane checked the man's chest and abdomen, his arms and legs.

"I don't think the blood's from him."

"Thank God," she breathed again, then thought of another terrible possibility. The blood could be from Grant Davis. But she didn't say that now, not when they were focused on President Stack.

Shane touched the man's cool skin and looked down at the shallow rise and fall of his chest. "He's not injured, but he's unconscious. I think they drugged him."

Ariana came down on her knees on the other side of the president and took his limp hand, squeezing and chafing it as she spoke quietly to him.

"President Stack? You're all right. We've found you. You're safe now."

When he didn't answer, she kept speaking. "President Stack, you're safe. Everything is all right. Wake up."

Shane's methods were a bit more aggressive. He shook the president's shoulders. When he didn't respond, he slapped him across the face.

Ariana winced.

But it worked. Stack's eyes fluttered open, then filled with alarm as he focused on the shape hovering over him. The president surged off the step and reached out a shaky arm toward Shane.

"Sir, take it easy," Shane soothed. "You're all right. We found you on the back steps at the Hancock Tower. Just a few floors down from the reception room. The kidnappers are gone."

"You..." His voice trailed off. Then he cleared his throat. "I'm sorry I lunged at you."

"Understandable."

The president sat down and continued to study Shane. "You're not one of them. One of the men who hustled us out of the room," he said, his voice slightly slurred.

"No. I'm Shane Peters."

It was amazing how quickly the president's thought processes clicked into place. "The security expert."

"Yes. And this is…" Shane started to say.

President Stack turned to her, then finished the sentence for Shane. "Princess Ariana of Beau Pays."

The man tried to stand up, but Shane kept a hand on his shoulder, holding him down. "Don't try to do too much yet. Tell me what happened to you."

"They separated me and Davis from the crowd. After we went down a couple of flights of stairs, they stuck a hypodermic into my arm, through my jacket and shirt, and I conked out."

"You need to be checked by a doctor."

Ignoring Shane, the president looked around. "Where's Vice President Davis?"

"I'm sorry, sir. He appears to be missing."

"They took Davis and left me?" he said, sounding puzzled by the scenario.

"It looks like it. Do you know why?" Shane pressed. He had a pretty good idea why, but he wanted to hear what the president thought.

"They didn't say. But the whole time we were together, they seemed more interested in Davis than me." He closed his eyes for a moment.

"Are you dizzy?" Shane asked.

"Yes. Give me a moment."

When he opened his eyes again, he looked around

and saw the blood on the floor. "Oh, Lord, that could be from the vice president."

Shane responded quickly. "Did they shoot him? Hit him on the head? Head wounds bleed a lot, even if they're not serious."

"I don't know what they did to him! Or where they took him," President Stack answered in frustration. "Whatever happened, it was after I passed out."

"We'll get a sample of the blood to a crime lab," Shane answered.

The president grabbed the sleeve of Shane's tuxedo jacket. "I need to tell you something else," he muttered.

"What?" Shane asked, looking up and down the stairs.

"I know you were on your way down, trying to escape. But in the kitchen…they tied up two Secret Service agents. They may still be up there."

Shane looked up the steps again, and Ariana knew he was struggling with a dilemma. She had to provide him with a good way to make the decision.

Keeping her voice calm, she leaned over the president. "It's not safe for us to stay in the stairwell, but if you can stand, I can help you through the door into the hallway. Then Mr. Peters can go up and find out what's happening in the kitchen."

The president nodded.

Over his head, she and Shane exchanged glances. "Okay," he mouthed.

She and Shane helped President Stack to his feet. He wavered for several seconds, then gathered his strength together and stiffened his knees. Leaning on them heavily, he walked the few feet to the exit door, panting by the time they stepped into the corridor.

As President Stack rested against the wall, she saw Shane's doubtful expression, and she was afraid that the plan wouldn't work.

The president gave up the fight to look dignified and sank to the floor. Ariana came down beside him.

"I can't leave you," Shane muttered.

In the dim emergency light, Allan Stack's expression turned fierce. "Of course you can. The president of the United States orders you to go up and free those agents."

Chapter Eight

Shane wondered about the wisdom of abandoning Ariana with a man who had been drugged—even if he was the president of the United States.

But he was worried about the agents, too. He knew one of them was his friend Ty Jones.

With Ariana and the president outside the stairwell, they were unlikely to be found. The armed men who had hustled the president and vice president out of the reception area weren't coming back for President Stack. It was Davis they'd wanted. And they'd gotten him.

"I'll be back as soon as I can," Shane said. "Stay right here."

"Oui," Ariana promised.

Shane hurried back up the steps. Instead of taking the hallway he and Ariana had used to circle around from the front of the building, he turned directly toward the kitchen. The door was closed, and he was more cautious than he'd been at the entrance to the stairs, since the bad guys could be up here.

When he pressed his ear against the barrier, he heard nothing. Taking a chance, he eased the door open a crack. With only the emergency lighting functioning, it took several moments for him to take in the scene. Then he saw two men gagged and tied to chairs.

One of them was at the side of the kitchen, furiously sawing his bound wrists against the edge of the kitchen counter. Shane saw that it was Ty.

He called to his friend, and Ty's head jerked up, his eyes widening when he saw his Eclipse buddy. He tried to say something, but the gag in his mouth prevented speech.

Shane ran to Ty and saw that the rope that secured his wrists was partially cut. A few more minutes and he'd have freed himself.

Shane set down the fire extinguisher he was still holding and pulled out his plastic knife, using it to finish cutting the bonds on Ty's wrists. Then he removed the gag and ran over to the other man. It was Charlie Mercer, President Stack's Secret Service agent.

"The president?" he asked as soon as Shane had removed his gag.

"President Stack is okay," he said. "We found him two floors down."

"We?" Mercer asked as Shane cut through the rope on his wrists.

"I left him with Princess Ariana. They're not in the stairwell. We moved the president to the hallway."

"You got the princess out of the reception room?" Ty asked.

"Yes."

"Way to go." Then his face sobered. "What about Vice President Davis?"

"I'm sorry. We didn't find him. Only the president."

"Do you have a phone?" Mercer asked urgently as soon as his hands were free.

"Yes." Shane pulled out the cell phone and handed it over.

The Secret Service agent immediately began punching in numbers. Seconds later, he apprised his counterparts on the ground of the new developments. When he finished, he looked up. "We have all the exits to the building secured. And they're sending a helicopter for the president."

"Good," Ty answered, but he looked badly shaken, and Shane could imagine what he was feeling now. Vice President Davis was the responsibility of Ty Jones. And Davis was missing.

Logically, there was nothing Ty could have done to save the vice president, not when he was being held at gunpoint. But Shane knew that didn't make his friend feel any better. He hated giving Ty the next piece of news. "There's blood down on the stairs where we found the president. He wasn't wounded. If it's not from one of the bad guys, then Davis is the most likely source."

"Damn," Ty muttered.

"We'll get a crime-scene unit in here. They'll get a sample and find out," Mercer answered.

"There won't be any labs open in the city," Ty pointed out. "Not with the power off."

"Then they'll take it to the closest place that's open," Shane told him.

Mercer broke into their conversation. "You say the president wasn't wounded. But what's his condition?" As he spoke, he finished with the tape holding his ankles to the chair.

"He was conscious. But it looks like they gave him something to knock him out. He said it was some kind of injection."

"I'm going down there." Mercer pulled off the duct tape and dashed for the service entrance to the kitchen.

"Wait. One more thing," Shane advised him. "There was no cyanide gas at the front entrance to the reception area."

"And none at the back," Ty said. "Or we'd be dead now. Which means they were just faking that part of the scenario."

Ty and Shane exchanged glances, and he suspected they had both come to the same conclusion. The leader of the gunmen was Liam Shea. He'd set up a scenario as much like the Barik rescue mission as he could manage, and the gas had been included to remind Grant Davis and the other members of the team of that night of terror. Shea had also wanted to capture Davis, and apparently he had him.

"The hallway, right?" Mercer said before hurrying out of the room. Ty and Shane turned toward the kitchen door—the only barrier between them and two of the men who still held a roomful of people hostage.

"You going to tell your boss you think Liam Shea set this up?" he asked. "With the help of his sons."

"As soon as we get out of here."

"Can we take the bastards by surprise?" Ty asked.

"Risky. They've got machine guns, and we've got kitchen knives."

Just as they turned to look around for more effective weapons, the door burst open.

Knife in hand, Shane whirled toward the door. He and Ty found themselves face-to-face with a lean man with gray hair and wild eyes.

It was the oil-company executive Shane had seen at the beginning of the evening.

"You're not them!" he croaked.

"Not the kidnappers? They're not out there?"

The executive shook his head. "They're gone. They told us that if we didn't stay in the reception area, we'd be gassed or shot. But then I heard you talking out here, and I thought you weren't them." He looked at Ty. "You're one of the Secret Service agents, right?"

"Yes."

"And you're the security guy," he said to Shane.

"Yeah." Shane turned to Ty. "It looks like the other two got away. I wonder how they did it."

"I can't believe they could get out of the building so fast." He looked at Shane. "We've got to tell the guys downstairs what's happened."

Shane pulled out his phone again and handed it to Ty. "And somebody's got to take charge up here. I think you're it. I have to get the princess out of harm's way."

"Maybe they'll send more helicopters for the rest of the dignitaries."

"That makes sense," Shane answered.

Ty called the forces on the ground to tell them the last two hostage takers had disappeared and that they needed medics in the reception area to treat the wounded.

Shane waited impatiently for the return of his phone. As soon as it was back in his hand, he exited through the back door and charged down the stairs.

When he bolted through the door to the fifty-eighth floor, he stopped short.

Ariana and the president weren't where he'd left them. Then he saw her peek around a corner and breathed out a sigh.

"They took President Stack down?" he asked.

"Yes. Agent Mercer took him. The president was leaning on him. I would have let him rest, but the agent wanted to get him out of here as quickly as possible."

"Yeah."

She shook her head. "He looks ten years older than when he gave that speech at the reception."

"Unfortunately," Shane agreed, then gave Ariana a news bulletin. "The last two of the bad guys left the crowd alone in the reception area and warned them not to move. The gunmen are gone."

"Thank God," she breathed.

"I'd like to know where they went," Shane muttered.

"Won't the police and the Secret Service search the building?" she asked.

"Of course. But it's the tallest building in New England, with a lot of places to hide. They could even have kept Vice President Davis in here." Switching topics, he said, "There's a helicopter coming for the president, and hopefully for the rest of the dignitaries."

The conversation was interrupted by the sound of men pounding up the stairs.

"Who's there?" Shane shouted, not that he could do much if it turned out to be the kidnappers.

"Boston PD."

"Did you meet a Secret Service agent and the president coming down?"

"Yes."

"What's the status of the blackout?" Shane asked.

"It's all over the city. Apparently explosive charges were set to detonate at several key power plants," the police detective said.

"How did they get in? You'd think there would be good security after 9/11."

"You'd think," the man agreed.

Shane shook his head. "Let me guess. The power company can't get the plants online anytime soon?"

"Right. They're estimating that it's going to take at least two days to get back online."

"Lucky Boston!"

Shane knew that with the whole city dysfunctional, it would be that much harder to find Grant Davis. Which was probably one of the reasons the kidnappers had gone to the trouble of blacking out the whole area, not just the Hancock Tower.

The men continued up the stairs, and Shane turned to Ariana. "Let's get out of here."

As they started down the stairs, another harsh reality was sinking in. He was never going to see her again.

He wanted to ask if she was regretting getting tangled up with him. Well, not the rescue part. The instant attraction between them that had led them both into forbidden territory.

But he wasn't going to mention the subject, if she didn't. After this ordeal, he was sure she'd want to get back to her country as soon as possible. He'd heard that she was engaged to marry someone. Some nobleman named Jacques or Claude or something like that. He wondered if she'd share the same kind of passion with her husband that she'd shared with him.

Just one kiss. Well, two if you counted the fooling around under the table in the reception room when he was trying to get her mind off the kidnappers.

He shouldn't be thinking about them.

Doggedly, he brought his mind back to the hostage situation. Two of the Sheas had taken the president and vice president out of the reception room. Two of them had stayed to control the hostages for a few more minutes, then had slipped out when they'd gotten some kind of all-clear signal. Or had they needed a signal?

Perhaps, given Liam Shea's bad luck with signals, they'd just left at a prearranged time.

He'd bet Shea had gone with Grant Davis. Shea and one of the boys. And the other two had stayed in the building and were hiding there somewhere. But where?

He'd studied Liam. He hadn't thought he needed to study the sons as well.

His mistake.

Beside him, Ariana cleared her throat. "When we get downstairs, we won't be able to…say anything personal."

"Yeah."

"I should thank you for saving my life."

"You're welcome," he said stiffly.

"I thought you were an upstart American," she added. "I was wrong about you. You're one of the most accomplished men I've ever met."

"You're going to give me a swelled head."

"Don't act modest. You know you're good in an emergency situation."

And are you going to tell me I'm good at kissing? he wondered, but didn't voice the thought.

They kept walking. He wanted to stop her and turn her to him. He wanted to find out what would happen if he pulled her into his arms again.

Would their passion flare up the way it had earlier? Or would she stiffen in his arms? He felt his stomach clench and kept putting one foot in front of the other.

She was a princess. As a kid, he'd scraped for everything he'd gotten. And some nights he'd gone to bed with a powdered juice drink for dinner because they'd run out of food.

He slid Ariana a sideways glance. Because he couldn't stand the idea of losing her, he searched around for a way to keep her talking. It was a long way down from the top floor. That gave him the opportunity to find out a lot about her.

"Tell me about Beau Pays," he said.

"It's beautiful." She laughed. "Of course, that's what the name means. Beautiful country."

"Yeah."

"I guess it was a nice place to grow up."

Her voice took on a glow. "Yes. Our largest city has a population of only three hundred thousand. So people can get around without cars a lot of the time. That cuts down on pollution. But at the same time, we're very cosmopolitan. Tourism is one of our chief industries. So we have wonderful restaurants, a theater festival every summer, great resorts with summer hiking and winter skiing."

"And the architecture looks like an Alpine village?"

"Not in the city. It's very old European. Like Paris or maybe Vienna. With lots of ornamentation on the buildings."

"Where did you live?"

She hesitated for a moment. "We have a house in town and one out in the country."

"Are you embarrassed to call it a palace?"

She shrugged. "I guess you could call it that. But it's not on the scale of Versailles or Windsor. You'd probably just think of them as nice country houses."

Yeah, sure, he thought. A nice little mansion. With a reception room, grand ballroom, opulent bedrooms and servants' quarters. But he didn't contradict her.

"We didn't need anything like a fortress because the mountains would have made an invasion difficult."

She gave him a quick glance, then looked away. "Did you see *The Sound of Music?*"

"Yes."

"You know that first shot, where Julie Andrews is up on the mountain in the sunshine? My childhood surroundings looked a lot like that."

"And everybody in your country is a fantastic singer?"

She started to answer, then got the joke and laughed. "I can't carry a tune, actually."

"Despite the best efforts of your tutors?"

"I did have a lot of lessons. Fencing. Dancing. Art. I'm pretty good at watercolors."

"I'd like to see some," he said before he realized that was highly unlikely.

She didn't speak, and he was sorry he'd brought up their seeing each other again.

"Is it hard being a princess?" he finally asked.

"My early life was kind of a balancing act. On the one hand, my father wanted us to have a normal upbringing, so we went to school with other children, then to top boarding schools. Our summers were busy, too. My father had me and my brother going to state functions when we were still in grade school."

"Your brother?"

He heard her swallow and knew he'd stepped into another subject he should have realized was a bad idea.

"He died four years ago. In a skiing accident."

"I'm sorry."

"It was a terrible blow to my father. And it meant that I became the heir to the throne."

"That shifted a lot of responsibility to you."

"Yes."

He tried to imagine what her life would have been like—and what it would be like in the future. He lived in a society that admired the rich and famous, which was why he'd always kept a low profile himself. She'd put a good face on being her royal highness, but he figured it must have been like living in a gilded cage.

They reached the ground floor and crossed the large lobby, then exited through one of the revolving doors and stepped outside.

Both of them stopped short, taking deep breaths of the night air as they stood under the long curved porch that sheltered the entrance to the building.

When he'd come in, he'd admired the mounds of impatiens and hostas in the raised planter boxes that bordered the plaza in front of the building. Now he saw the five-foot-high polished granite planters with new eyes. Of course, they were barriers designed to protect the courtyard.

Earlier in the evening, there had been a few policemen and Secret Service agents in the plaza. Since the blackout, a small army had gathered at the base of the building. National Guard troops, Secret Service men and police filled the space. In the street beyond he caught glimpses of emergency vehicles—police cars, ambulances, fire engines—and also some of the limousines that had been waiting for the partygoers upstairs.

Trucks from television stations were also part of the mix, although the police were keeping the media well away from the entrance. When a security detail approached, Ariana waved them away.

"Are we on television?" she asked, glaring at the media.

"Probably."

"So much for privacy," she said as she bent down and put her shoes back on, then straightened to pat at her hair. It had been carefully coiffed into an elegant up-sweep for the reception. The past few hours had loosened the coiffure, creating a charming disorder of misplaced strands that caressed her neck and cheeks.

As if she had followed his thoughts, she touched her hair. "How do I look?" she asked.

"Beautiful." Then he realized that he'd probably given too much away. "Nobody is going to expect you to look like you stepped out of a diplomatic reception," he added quickly.

"Didn't I?"

They shared a sharp laugh, then both went very still, staring at each other in a little bubble of space that isolated them from the rest of the world. They were standing a few feet apart, but it might as well have been a thousand miles.

The sound of a helicopter landing shattered the air above them and the protective bubble.

Beyond the immediate vicinity of the building, he could hear cars honking and people shouting at each other. The chaos was punctuated by the distant sound of breaking glass, and he pictured someone smashing a shop window across the square on Boylston Street.

In the distance he heard gunshots. And he knew that as soon as they stepped out into the plaza, they would enter a no-man's-land.

A uniformed cop came up to them and checked Shane's I.D.

"I don't have I.D.," Ariana said.

"I was told you were coming down, Your Highness. This way. We'll be taking off from Copley Square."

Shane looked toward the square and saw uniforms stationed every few yards along the route they would be taking.

"We'd better go."

Shane ushered Ariana around the side of the building and into St. James Avenue, the short street that separated the Hancock Tower from the open square.

In a war zone, it always struck him how thin the veneer of civilization was. As they stepped into the street, it felt like staid old Boston had disintegrated to that level.

Footsteps made them both whirl. A Secret Service agent came up to them and addressed Ariana. "A chopper will be landing shortly. It will be leaving from the center of the grassy area over there, just as soon as some of the others make it to the first floor." He looked at Shane. "Will you escort her over?"

"Of course."

"Appreciate it," the agent answered, and Shane knew the man had his hands full.

Before the agent could trot off, Ariana asked, "What about the injured?"

"They're being taken to local hospitals with emergency power."

"How many dead?" Shane asked, then was sorry he'd brought up the subject in front of Ariana.

"Eight."

He winced.

"Including Manfred," she whispered.

"I'm sorry."

"Where is the helicopter going?" Ariana asked.

"Otis Air Force Base."

The finality of the answer tore at Shane. They'd had

a horrible night in Boston, yet now that it was almost over, he didn't want it to end.

ARIANA SAW THE GRIM set of his features. She wondered if her face looked as tight and set.

"This way," he said, his voice sounding as stiff as his features. She'd like to know what he was thinking, but she couldn't ask him. Because what would she do with the answer when he gave it to her?

Did he wish he could keep up the relationship with her?

What relationship?

Under normal circumstances, it would be laughable to even think in those terms. She'd known the man less than two hours, but it felt as if they'd spent half a lifetime with each other, because almost every moment of their time together had taken place inside a pressure cooker. From their first dance to the wild kiss in the hallway.

As she contemplated that kiss, she wondered if she could ask him to visit her in Beau Pays. But where would that lead? She was engaged to be married to someone else. She could hardly spend a lot of time with Shane Peters. Even if she did, it would only be postponing the break with him. And was she really thinking that they could go off alone somewhere together?

They had no past together beyond this blazingly intense night. And no future. She knew that as well as she knew her duty to her country.

She was all about duty and self-sacrifice, just like her father and her mother, two people who had a comfortable, polite marriage but nothing like the fairy-tale love matches she had read about in books. And where did love get you if you got tangled up with a royal? Princess Diana had thought she was marrying into a fairy-tale existence, and look how she had ended up.

Automatically, Ariana followed along beside Shane, not really looking where they were going.

As they started across the street, he suddenly grabbed her arm, and she gasped.

"What?"

He pulled her back against his body as a car careened past them, weaving among the emergency vehicles.

With his hand firmly against her back, he moved her to the sidewalk, then into the shadows of a black van that was parked at the curb.

Still holding her close, he asked, "Are you all right?"

She swallowed, then laid her head against his broad shoulder. "No," she whispered.

"Are you hurt?" he asked anxiously, his hands moving up and down her back.

"No."

"Then what?"

All her past experience and training urged her to simply turn away and go to the helicopter landing area. Instead, she heard herself say, "If you can't figure it out, then forget it."

Shane's hands tightened around her, gathering her closer. "I think I can figure it out."

They stood close, and she nestled against him as he stroked up and down her back. If she turned her face up, she knew their lips would meet. She wanted that so much. Wanted to taste him, feel his mouth moving against hers with the urgency of that explosive moment in the hall.

Then she remembered they were out on the street, with a dozen TV cameras somewhere nearby.

She didn't give a damn if somebody spotted her with Shane Peters. But she knew her father would care. Very much. He'd set standards for the heir to the throne of Beau Pays, and she had always honored those standards. Until tonight.

"We can't stay here," she said.

"Yeah."

He looked out into the street. This time it seemed clear, and he led her across and into the shadows of a green striped awning set up along the side of Copley Square.

More awnings stood on either side of it.

"What are these for?" she asked.

"There's a street market here."

"Very charming," she answered, then immediately thought how inane that must sound.

At the end of the square, the Secret Service or the police had set up generator-powered floodlights. Presumably, the police had closed the square, because it was now empty. She saw yellow tape at the far side.

Shane led her toward the lit area as a helicopter took off.

"I guess the president is safely out of here," she whispered. *"Dieu merci."*

"Agreed."

She looked up and down the square. A large stone church was at one end and a massive public structure was across the street at the other end.

"What's that building?" she asked, not because she really needed to know, but because she wanted to keep hearing Shane's voice.

"The Boston Public Library," he answered.

"It's big."

"I guess it's a city of readers."

As the chopper disappeared into the darkness, she heard the sound of another one arriving. Gracefully it set down in the pool of lights.

"Your ride's here," he said. "It's a Sikorsky Seahorse. A good little machine."

"Uh-huh." Apparently he was up on his helicopters, or he was doing the same thing as she was—manufacturing conversation.

The helicopter came down low, hardly touching the ground.

"It's maintaining upward lift power," he said. "Ready for a dust off."

"Which is?"

"A quick takeoff. Better hurry or it will leave without you. It only holds twelve, including the crew."

As he spoke, she realized that this was the last time she was going to see him. "I wish I didn't have to leave."

She heard him swallow in the darkness, felt the touch of his hand on her bare arm. "I'd ask you to stay, if I thought it would do either one of us any good."

Her heart squeezed painfully. Because tears stung her eyes, and she didn't want him to see them, she turned away and started toward the center of the square, toward the temporary landing pad.

But she wasn't the only one who was trying to get out of Boston as quickly as possible after hours of terror up at the reception. As she hurried toward the lit area, other elegantly dressed people emerged from the shadows, and she recognized them from the reception.

She felt the wind coming off the blades as they approached the machine, and fought the universal impulse to duck.

Shane waited until the door swung open. Two people rushed past and scrambled inside.

"Why didn't they send a bigger helicopter?" the woman shouted above the noise of the rotors.

"Luck of the draw," Shane answered, although it looked as if he might as well have saved his breath as the woman pushed past him.

Ariana still didn't climb aboard. She wondered if she'd miss the flight if she held back.

"I'll help you up," Shane said, climbing into the doorway.

"Help the older people in," she said.

He offered his hand to an elderly man, then a woman who looked as if she'd lived through a world war. And finally it was Ariana's turn, if she wanted to get out of here.

She had thought she did. Now she was so torn.

As Shane leaned over to give her his hand, something solid and heavy tumbled out from under the sleeve of his jacket and clattered to the ground.

When she looked down, she gasped.

In the illumination from the floodlights, she saw what had fallen. It was the Beau Pays sapphire.

Chapter Nine

Stunned, Ariana stared at the gem glittering in the flood-lights. In one smooth motion, she jumped down from the helicopter and scooped up the priceless sapphire. Holding it in her fist, she raised her eyes to Shane's.

Before either one of them could speak, a woman dashed out of the shadows and made for the chopper. Pushing past Ariana, she scrambled through the open doorway.

"I have a full load. You'll have to wait for the next chopper," the pilot called above the noise of the rotor.

The blades set up a whirlwind around Ariana as Shane pulled her away from the machine lifting off. As it disappeared into the blackness, they were left standing at the edge of the lit area staring at each other.

"Where did you get this?" she gasped, holding up the gem and waving it in his face.

"I…"

"Answer me!" she spat out. "And don't tell me that in the middle of that madhouse up there, you decided to rescue my family's most prized posses-sion. If you'd done that, you would have mentioned it to me before now."

"I took it before the shooting started." Before she could make an appropriate comment, he went on quickly. "To prove your security was a joke."

She could barely contain her anger enough to speak coherently. But she managed to say, "Let's get the time frame straight. Did you steal it before we danced?" she inquired, her voice dangerously calm.

"Yes."

"You expect me to believe that you had my family's best interests at heart—my best interests at heart?"

"It's the truth."

The enormity of his betrayal hit her like a cannonball striking her chest. "I let you kiss me," she choked out. "You must have been laughing the whole time."

"No."

"Then what?"

"I was…blown away by that kiss."

"Don't make it worse." She couldn't stand the sight of this man who had taken advantage of her as though she were some naive little debutante who didn't know any better. He was a smug opportunist who had manipulated her emotions, and if she stayed near him another moment, she would throw up.

Too bad she'd lost her place on the helicopter.

She didn't know when another one was coming, and she was hardly capable of rational thought at the moment.

As she stood in the spotlight, a cracking sound split the air and something whizzed past her head.

Beside her, Shane swore. "Someone's shooting at you. Get out of the light," he shouted.

"Shooting? Out here?"

"Yes. Get down." As he tugged at her arm, she tried

to make sense of the words. They'd escaped from the madhouse at the top of the Hancock Tower. They should be safe. But the nightmare wasn't over.

She wrenched away from the man who had played on her emotions so skillfully. She might be in danger, but she still couldn't stomach Shane Peters's touch.

Behind her, more gunfire sounded.

"Get the hell out of the light," he said again.

Whirling toward the edge of the square, she began to run. She didn't know the area. She didn't know the city. But she knew that she had to get to the cover of darkness.

Shane was right behind her, keeping pace. And it registered somewhere in her mind that he was shielding her back from the gunfire.

As she dashed into the darkness, she almost tripped over her long skirt. Reaching down, she hiked it up, holding it in one hand as she kept going.

"This way," Shane shouted.

"Get away from me."

As she ran, she tried to form a vague plan. She'd seen a lot of police officers. She would find one of them. Once she was out of danger, she would have Shane Peters arrested for stealing the sapphire.

Maybe he'd talk his way out of it. But she'd still have the gem.

The skirt was out of the way, but her high heels sank into the grass. She wanted to take them off again, but now she was clutching the sapphire in her free hand. So she kept going as best she could, her breath coming in gasps.

Ahead of her she saw two brass statues that made her blink. The hare and the tortoise—with the rabbit stopping to scratch its ear and the tortoise in the lead.

The absurdity of finding them here—in this situation—would have made her laugh, if she'd had the breath to spare.

Before she reached the statues, another shot rang out. Then another.

Behind her, Shane cursed. This time, when his hand shot out, he dragged her onto the grass. Somehow she managed to hang on to the sapphire as she hit the flat surface.

"Get off of me," she sputtered.

"Do you want to get killed?"

Shane took her free hand, pulling her toward a flower bed, then around it and onto the pavement along the side of the square.

Another statue loomed in front of them, this one much larger. It was a man in old-fashioned buckled shoes, tights and a frock coat. Shane shoved her unceremoniously behind the base of the statue.

"John Copley's not going to give us much cover," he muttered.

Ariana stood there, leaning against the granite slab and sucking in air.

Peters was taking charge again. And much as she hated to admit it, he seemed like her best hope for survival.

When he looked to his left and right, she did the same. Down at one end of the square was a round kiosk. At the other end were low stone walls. Looming above them and glowing in the moonlight, she saw two pillars that looked like small versions of the Washington Monument.

"Come on."

"Where?"

"The side of the fountain."

"Those monuments are part of a fountain?"

"Yeah. Go."

As she headed for the low granite wall, Shane covered her back again. More bullets pinged into the polished stone. After ducking behind the wall, she looked toward the flashes of muzzle fire and caught a glimpse of a guy wearing dark coveralls.

"Who?" she gasped.

"Maybe one of the men from upstairs. But he's taken off his waiter's outfit."

She tried to wrap her head around that. "But why would he come after us down here?"

"They singled you out before. Now they're after you again. We have to find better cover. And we're going to have to crawl again. Give me the sapphire."

Her head jerked toward him. "You must be crazy."

"You can't crawl and hold the damn thing."

Her hand closed around the jewel.

"Don't let your anger at me get you killed," he bit out as he pried her fingers from around the priceless jewel and took it away.

She might have screamed at him to return her property, but a bullet hit the sidewalk to their left. Another hit one of the slender monuments.

Shane's voice grounded her. "I know you hate me," he said, his tone as flat as a sheet of glass. "But I'm trying to save your life. Stay down and move to your right, so the fountain blocks the shooter's view. Make for the side of the church."

"Where is it?"

"Straight ahead. Use the flower bed as cover. They won't stop any bullets, but they'll hide you."

"Okay," she agreed.

COLIN SHEA STARED AT THE EDGE of the weird-looking fountain with its twin monument towers and horizontal waterspouts.

Whoever had designed the monstrosity should be shot.

Like the fairy-tale princess and her good buddy.

They were using the side of the fountain for cover, but they'd left their backs exposed. If he could get behind them, he could nail them.

Colin moved through the shadows, angling around to the other side of the square.

He'd seen the princess and Shane Peters dancing early in the evening, looking as if they wanted to find a room. Then, when the fun had started, he'd lost track of them. For all he knew, they could have been boinking each other in a broom closet while his family had been terrorizing the partygoers. Maybe that was what they *had* been doing, since they'd disappeared from view.

Right now, it looked as if they weren't so tight. The Secret Service agent had told her to get on the helicopter. And she'd almost gotten away. Then the fumbling security guy had dropped her precious sapphire, and she'd gone bananas.

Which was lucky for Colin because he'd gotten another crack at her. His brother Finn had told him about going to scoop up the sapphire and finding it missing.

They'd agreed that Peters must have taken it. And then the stupid jerk had dropped it—right at the feet of the princess.

So now Colin was going to get Peters, the sapphire and the princess. Three for one—not a bad deal. And the last two were the best because they'd bring the high-and-mighty Frederick LeBron, king of Beau Pays, to his knees.

The guy might be the ruler of his dinky little kingdom now. But Dad had told them how LeBron had acted on that mission to Barik. He'd pretended he was one of the guys, just an ordinary Arab-language interpreter assigned to the rescue team.

But really he'd made sure you knew he was the future king of Beau Pays. Well, he was about to pay for his arrogance tonight. And if he was the guy who had given the signal too early to Dad, then he'd get what he deserved for that, too.

Colin rounded the corner of the fountain and brought his Glock into position, then stopped short. He'd anticipated a clear shot at the little princess and her stand-in bodyguard. But they were gone. Where the hell could they have disappeared out here in the open square?

On foot, they couldn't be far away. But he'd better find them before they got out of Copley Square and disappeared into the city.

ARIANA KEPT MOVING, conscious that Shane was behind her. He could have taken the lead, but he was still at her back, shielding her from the gunfire.

As she dodged around a decorative metal fence and into a flower bed, she let out a sigh of relief. At least they weren't so exposed now. But the man might still spot them.

"I don't like it, but we may have to take our chances in the city," Shane whispered.

Across the street, she heard the sound of more breaking glass.

"Looters," Shane muttered. "That's a high-end shopping district over there. I guess some upstanding Boston citizens are loading up on Gucci bags and Hermès scarves."

She started to move forward again when a figure emerged from the shadows, and she gasped.

"Hands where I can see them. Don't move," a rough voice commanded.

"Who are you?" Shane challenged.

"FBI Agent Ben Parker."

Ariana froze. Beside her, Shane did the same thing. But he let out a sigh of relief. "We're not the bad guys. It's Shane Peters and Ariana LeBron."

A flashlight beam hit her in the face, and she lifted an arm to shield her eyes. The beam moved on, sweeping over the man next to her on the ground.

"Shane? What the hell are you doing out here? I thought you were escorting the princess to the chopper coming for the dignitaries."

"That was the mission. But we had a little…mishap," he finished. "Somebody's shooting at us."

"Who?"

"In the dark, it's hard to tell. It could be one of the killers from up in the tower."

"He's not shooting now."

"Maybe because you're armed," Shane answered.

"Yeah. Well, there's only one of me. Get into the church. I'll hold him off if I have to."

Before she left the cover of the flower bed, Ariana looked directly at the man who had stopped them. "You're FBI?" she confirmed, thinking she could accomplish two purposes at once—getting to safety and getting away from Shane Peters.

Immediately, he whipped out a badge and shone his light on it.

After studying it, she asked, "Can't I stay with you?"

"No. I'm on duty, patrolling this part of the square. I'm supposed to keep the hoi polloi away until we get the guests out of here. And I don't want to be responsible for losing a princess, so get into the church."

Shane cut into the exchange. "Come on," he said, his voice gritty.

She looked up at the massive stone building looming in the dark. She couldn't see it well now, but she remembered studying it much earlier in the evening, when she'd first gotten out of her limousine, because it was such a unique combination of high Victorian Gothic and French Romanesque architecture.

Mon Dieu.

She had to suppress a hysterical laugh. She was running for her life, with a man who turned her stomach, and she was thinking about the architecture class she'd taken at the Sorbonne.

Or maybe it was easier for her mind to cope with architecture than Shane's betrayal and the specter of her own death out here in the middle of a Boston park.

The church was right across the street from the Hancock Tower. Apparently, as they'd dodged their way around the square, trying to avoid getting killed, they'd come back to near their starting position.

"Why not go back where we came from?" she asked.

The FBI agent answered promptly. "You might run right into the guys who took you hostage in the first place since we don't know where they are."

She nodded, then ran toward the heavy archway at

the front of the church where the shadows were darker than in the square.

She couldn't see the gargoyles above her head, but she could make out steps and a ramp leading up to massive front doors.

Shouldn't they be locked?

Shane reached her side and pushed on one of the doors. It swung inward. When she peered through the opening, she saw more darkness.

"Come on." He stepped into the narthex—the vestibule at the back of the sanctuary—and almost immediately bumped into a small, high table or stand that someone had set there. It must have held some kind of papers, because they cascaded onto the tile floor.

She heard him repress a comment that she suspected wasn't appropriate for a house of worship.

"What was that?"

"I don't know."

He switched on a small flashlight, playing it over the mess they'd made.

"Brochures. It looks like they have the weekly schedule of activities."

"Where did you get the flashlight?"

"I'm always prepared. Didn't I tell you I was a Boy Scout?" he asked.

"That's hard to believe," she answered, then turned toward him in the darkness. She'd agreed to come in here, but that didn't mean she had to stay. Her voice was icy as she said, "I want you to take me to a police station. I'll call my father from there. And I want my sapphire back."

"As soon as we're safe, I'll give it to you. Right now, move away from the door."

"Who are you to order me around?"

"I'm trying to save your life. You can scratch my eyes out later."

She huffed out a breath and strove for the royal calm that had always stood her in such good stead.

Peters might be a common thief, but at the moment he was her best hope for survival.

He stepped to the interior doors and pointed the flashlight up, and she caught glimpses of magnificent stained-glass windows and murals.

"We're too exposed in here. Let's take a look at the undercroft," he said, ushering her toward a flight of stairs that led downward.

She struggled to put her emotions on hold as she followed him down the dark stairway. At the bottom was a heavy door with a trefoil-shaped window in the center.

On the other side, they stepped into a lower lobby bathed in the soft glow of emergency lights. She saw a gift shop and a large open space with benches along the sides. In each corner of the room, massive granite pilings rose to the ceiling, like the bases of stepped pyramids.

At both sides of the space were wooden racks that held long poles, probably used to carry candles or crosses during the service.

Shane gathered up several and carried them along with him, then opened a door in an etched-glass wall.

"What are those for?" she asked.

"Maybe I can use them as spears."

Beyond the glass was a large room with coffee urns on tables in the middle.

"Still too wide open," he muttered.

They crossed to a corridor lined with small rooms. Too bad they all had window walls that gave a good view of the interior.

In one room were cardboard boxes of clothing and household items that looked as if they were intended for the poor.

Shane stopped short and looked at the boxes. "You need to change into something more practical."

Ariana looked at him. She'd been trying to keep her emotions in neutral. Now she wondered if he was trying to take advantage of her again. Maybe. But in truth, she'd had trouble running in an evening gown and high heels.

While Shane stepped into the room, she hovered in the doorway, watching as he began sorting through the clothing. He pulled out a navy button-down shirt and a pair of jeans.

"These should fit you."

"Wouldn't that be cooler?" she asked, pointing to a white T-shirt.

"Yeah. But dark clothes will hide us better."

"What were you—a cat burglar in your spare time?"

"No. But I'd prefer not to stand out like targets in a shooting gallery."

She winced, and he went back to the boxes, where he unearthed a pair of jeans that looked like his size.

He found an almost new pair of running shoes, and socks in the box next to them.

"Try these."

From the doorway, she gave him a long look. "I'm not getting undressed in front of you."

"I wouldn't dream of invading your privacy, Your Highness. But I don't want you getting lost."

"You think I'm going to run away?"

"Will you?"

"Right now you're the lesser of two evils," she snapped.

"I'll turn my back." As he spoke, he did just that.

She hardly trusted him, but she stepped into the room. While he was standing with his back to her, she reached around and unzipped her evening gown. Quickly she eased it over her breasts. Lowering the bodice left the whole top of her body exposed because the front of the gown had been equipped with its own bra.

The cool air in the church basement tightened her nipples. Embarrassed, she hurried to pull on the shirt Shane had given her and buttoned it. She wished she had a bra. But not one that had belonged to some other woman.

The jeans were a little too big. But they'd do, she decided as she zipped them up. She threw her evening clothes into one of the boxes.

Turning around, she realized suddenly that she hadn't thought to give Shane the same courtesy he'd given her. He wasn't as modest as she had been, and he was standing with his back to her, wearing only a pair of white cotton briefs.

She took in his almost naked body. It was fit and firm, with tight buttocks, long legs and broad, well-muscled shoulders. He pulled on the shirt. Then, as though he knew she was watching him, he pivoted to face her.

Her mouth went dry. "I…I'm sorry," she managed to whisper.

He nodded and reached for the jeans. Watching him

step into them was like watching a tantalizing striptease in reverse.

Pulling her gaze away from his body, she brought her mind back to business. She might not like him, but perhaps she could get some information out of him.

"I have the feeling you know who was shooting at us," she said.

"I don't know for sure. I can guess."

"Who?"

He kept his gaze steady. "It may go back to that rescue mission to Barik that your father and I were on eleven years ago."

"How?"

He finished zipping up his pants "Like everyone else on the team, your dad has some good memories and some bad ones. But, overall, the operation went terribly wrong."

"But you got most of the hostages out," she answered quickly.

He made a dismissive sound. "Lucky for us. We were supposed to be operating with split-second precision, but one of the men screwed up the timing. He cut the power too quickly. That threw everything else off. The insurgents were alerted to our presence and went on the counterattack. Some of the hostages got out of there, but some of them died." He gave her a long look. "Put on your shoes."

She'd been so caught up in his revelations that she'd forgotten to finish getting dressed. She sat down on a nearby chair and pulled on the shoes.

As she tied the first shoe, she said, "My father never told me anyone died."

"It probably wasn't one of his better moments."

She leaped up immediately, her hands on her hips. "Are you saying the mission failure was his fault?"

"Of course not. Technically, it was Liam Shea's fault. He was the man who cut the power too quickly. He was tried for insubordination and given a ten-year sentence."

She made a quick calculation. "That means he got out of jail a year ago."

"Yes. I wanted to keep track of him. But he dropped out of sight. I think he was setting up a revenge scenario, with his three sons helping him."

She struggled to wrap her head around the idea. "Why do you think that?"

Shane flexed his feet in his borrowed shoes. "Tonight has a lot of parallels with the mission to Barik."

"Like what exactly?"

"The blackout. The hostages. The cyanide gas. And the people. You heard the president say that the kidnappers seemed more interested in Grant Davis than in him?"

"Yes."

"Well, Davis was on the mission."

"The vice president was with you?"

"He was just an army officer then. One of the team. So was I. Also Ty Jones and my brother, Chase. Your father was our civilian interpreter. He was supposed to be here tonight, too. Only he couldn't come to the reception, so you're standing in for him. When was that decision made?"

"A few days ago."

"So when you showed up instead, they had to improvise."

"You're saying tonight is all about…punishing the other members of the team."

"Yeah."

She caught her breath, considering the implications. It was too monstrous. Too much to take in. If he was right, then Liam Shea had been making plans for a long time. Or was Peters spinning this story for his own purposes?

"Why should I believe you?" she demanded.

"Do you have a better explanation?"

"No. But you could be using that story to keep me close to you."

He made a rough sound. "Why would I do that?"

"Why did you take the sapphire?"

"I told you my thinking on that."

She made an unladylike sound. "You gave me a crazy story about stealing it to prove our security system was inadequate."

"That's right. It was. You saw the proof."

She tipped her head to one side, studying him. "Is that how you get all your jobs—by subterfuge?"

"Of course not," he answered, his voice hard and quick in the darkened room.

He had hurt her. Under ordinary circumstances, she would simply have turned her back on him and walked away, and she would have made him believe he had never touched her emotions. But they were stuck in this little room, and she heard herself saying, "I guess you get a charge out of toying with people's feelings."

"No, I don't."

His denial only sparked her anger. "Oh come on. You were seeing how far you could play me, weren't you?"

Ariana watched Shane's expression turn stony, and all at once she knew she had pushed him too far.

She'd succeeded in putting herself into a dangerous situation without half trying.

Chapter Ten

Ariana's pulse pounded as the man she'd hated took a step forward, looming over her in the darkness.

"Are you saying that what happened between us wasn't real? Are you saying that I was playing some kind of game when I kissed you? That I wasn't emotionally involved?" he asked in a deceptively even voice.

Her mouth had turned so dry that she could hardly speak. She licked her lips, wondering what she was going to say and wondering if she had secretly been provoking him because she couldn't stand the gulf between them.

He was speaking again, the sound barely coming to her above the buzzing in her own ears.

"I think I've taken enough of your verbal abuse. Let's see if that's what you really think."

Before she could answer, he crossed the remainder of the space between them and took her in his arms.

She might have tried to push him away, but she was too stunned. He tipped her chin up and brought his mouth down on hers.

Their last kiss had been frantic. She might have called this one savage—if she'd been able to define it.

But she was hardly able to think. As Shane's mouth moved over hers, he swept her up in a whirlwind of feelings and sensations that had been simmering below the surface all the time they'd been together.

Anger hadn't wiped them away. Perhaps anger had intensified her response. Or perhaps she had been desperate to find out what had really happened between them.

Whatever it was ran strong and deep. She was instantly aroused. Instantly so needy that her knees went weak.

When he silently asked her to open for him, she was helpless to refuse. Her lips parted, and his tongue swept into her mouth, melding with her, the contact unbearably erotic.

He lifted his mouth a fraction of an inch. "You think *this* is playing?"

Honesty forced her to say "No."

"Thank God."

The emotion in his words made her sway on her feet. She had to cling to him to stay erect, and when she felt him sway, too, she sensed that he was as overcome as she was by the intimate contact and by the honesty of her answer.

He moved back, bringing her with him, bracing himself against the wall as he pulled her more firmly against his hard body.

He lowered his head again, and as he kissed her, his hands moved across her shoulders and into her hair, destroying what was left of her carefully arranged coiffure, sending her long hair cascading down her back.

She heard a moaning sound and knew that it had risen in her own throat.

He spoke her name, spoke directly into her mouth. And that was unbearably erotic.

She answered, helpless to do anything besides respond to this man she should never have met.

He shouldn't be holding her, kissing her. He shouldn't be reaching under her shirt, splaying his hands against the hot skin of her back.

But he was doing it, and she was letting him. More than letting him, she was reveling in the caress.

His hands moved restlessly across her back, then stopped.

"You're not wearing a bra!"

"It was part of my dress," she answered, hearing the embarrassment in her voice.

"Don't apologize. You feel wonderful. Your skin is so soft. Like warm silk."

His hands moved to her ribs, and when she didn't stop him, they traveled higher, to the sides of her breasts.

She made a strangled sound as he stroked her there, making her nipples contract to tight points of sensation.

"You like that."

"Yes."

Slowly, tenderly, giving her time to pull away, he moved his hands inward so that he could cup her breasts in his palms.

"Oh!"

No man had touched her so intimately. Ever. She had never imagined that it could feel so good.

She wanted more, but she didn't know what to ask for.

He stared down into her face as he glided his fingertips across the crests, creating powerful sensations in her body.

Her breath caught. So did his. She could feel a hard shaft pressing against her middle. She knew what it was. And she knew where this could lead.

"You feel so good," he whispered. "Which is why I have to stop."

He pulled his hands away, letting them drop to his sides.

"Don't," she pleaded.

"We both know we can't go any further."

She knew it, somewhere in her fogged brain. She felt as if she'd drunk too much champagne at a state reception. Still, she was astonished that she had let him go this far. Astonished that she had practically begged for him to do anything he wanted. Anything she wanted.

Her blood was on fire, and she didn't want to stop. Yet she knew that there were things that Princess Ariana of Beau Pays couldn't do. Must not do.

None of her training had prepared her for this situation. She shouldn't be here alone with a man. A man she wanted to make love with her. When she had read about scenes like this in books, she had thought they were just from the writer's imagination, certainly never thought they would apply to her.

"I'm sorry," Shane said.

"Don't be."

"I was taking advantage of you."

Only the truth would do. "Of course not." She stared at him and licked her lips. "You would never have gotten that far if I didn't want it."

"Okay."

The strained sound of his voice told her that he was serious about stopping. She couldn't stand that. Not yet. Even when she understood that there was a limit to how far she could take this.

She cleared her throat. Before she could stop herself, she said, "I heard two of the maids talking once…" She ran out of words and almost lost her nerve, then started again. "One of them said she told her boyfriend that they could do anything they wanted as long as they kept their jeans on."

His laugh was low and throaty. "Oh yeah? You mean you want to torture both of us?"

"Is it torture?" she asked in a small voice, knowing she was at a terrible disadvantage in this situation. Man-woman relationships were part of his background, but she didn't know the rules of this game. She only knew that she couldn't step away from him. Not now. She had to find a way to stay close to him.

She heard his answer, low and warm. "I think I can take it." He leaned back against the wall again, this time splaying his legs to equalize their heights before pulling her center against the fly of his jeans.

She closed her eyes as she felt his arousal straining behind the fabric. His hands went to her back, then slid lower, caressing her through the worn fabric of the jeans.

All her life, she'd been warned not to get herself into compromising situations. All her training told her that this was a dangerous game. She had been warned about men who would try to take advantage of her. But she didn't fear that with Shane. He had regained her trust, and she knew that he would drop his hands away from her body the moment she asked.

But she wasn't asking for him to stop. Not at all, even when the intimacy of his touch shocked her.

She made small, strangled sounds as he caressed her, his fingers stroking forbidden places, tracing the crack of her bottom, all the time moving her against his body.

Heat surged inside her. One of his hands slipped under her shirt again, finding her breast, playing with the nipple as his other hand swayed her lower body against his, creating wonderful friction.

She understood the physical sensations she was feeling, marveling at what he was doing to increase her pleasure.

The part of her that had always been a good girl screamed at her that she should pull away from him before it was too late. But she didn't want to pull away. She wanted the hot sensations to carry her up and up.

Unable to stop herself, she moved frantically against him, frustrated by the layers of fabric and yet sensing that they wouldn't keep her from reaching the peak of pleasure.

He bent his head, his breath hot on her ear as he whispered low, arousing words to her.

"You are so sexy. So sweet. I love seeing you like this. Feeling you moving against me. Knowing I'm making you unbearably hot."

She couldn't stop herself now. Her need was too strong, too urgent. She came undone in a blaze of sensation, pressing her mouth against his shoulder to muffle the cry that sprang to her lips as she rocked against him.

He gripped her shoulder, steadying her.

Her eyes blinked open, and she stared up at him, stunned that she had let herself go so far, and stunned that he had encouraged her.

In all the warnings she'd been given, nobody had ever mentioned anything like this.

COLIN SHEA STEPPED from the darkness of the square into the darker shadows under the church porch. The front door was ajar. Cautiously he approached the opening. This could be an ambush, and he wasn't going to let himself get trapped.

He poked his weapon inside, then swiftly rounded the corner. The vestibule was empty, but he saw evidence that someone had been through and made a mess. Apparently they had been in too much of a hurry to clean up.

A little table near the door was sitting catty wumpus in the aisleway, with brochures spilled onto the tile floor. Colin didn't think the janitor had left them lying there.

Too bad the floor was so clean otherwise. If there had been any dust, he might have seen a trail of footprints leading away from the entrance.

Okay, where was there to go in this place?

He looked around and saw that there were stairs at either end of the vestibule. He moved toward one set and stood at the top, listening intently.

He heard nothing, so he started cautiously down. At the bottom, he opened a door and stepped into an open area with a gift shop at one side.

It probably led to a dead end. Peters wouldn't be stupid enough to go in there.

Across from the gift shop was a glass wall with tall glass doors. He cautiously pulled one open and stepped into another large room.

Beyond was a hallway. Was it his imagination, or

could he hear heavy breathing down on the lower level, like someone was exercising hard?

Or doing something else that wasn't appropriate for a house of worship.

He held back a laugh. Score one for Peters. It sounded like he was having fun. Well, it was the last fun he was going to have.

In the square, Peters hadn't returned fire. Which meant he'd been unarmed outside. And it was highly unlikely that he'd acquired a weapon in the church.

Killing him and the princess was going to be like shooting fish under a bridge on the Charles River. With military precision, he slid a new clip into his own weapon, then started across the open space.

ARIANA'S BREATH WAS still racing. So was Shane's, and when she pressed her hand against his chest, she felt his heart thumping like a jackhammer.

"I…shouldn't…have…done that," she murmured, glad that the darkness hid the flush that spread across her cheeks.

He stroked his hand tenderly against her cheek. "If I'd wanted to stop you, I could have," he answered in a gritty voice. "But I wanted to have that to remember."

The words might be true, but the sound of loss in his voice made her chest tighten. When she tipped her head down, she found herself staring at the rigid flesh behind the fly of his jeans.

He'd spoken of torture. It hadn't been torture for her, but she knew she had left him hot and wanting. "What about you?" she said in a small voice.

"I'll survive," he clipped out.

Would she? She wasn't talking about physical satisfaction but emotional needs. She'd always known her role in life, always known that she must put her country before herself. That had helped her keep her emotions in check when she needed to focus on each job in her list of royal duties.

Suddenly, with this man, she felt as if blinders had been lifted off her eyes, and she was viewing the world in a whole new way. A dangerous way.

Even when she'd still been angry with him, she'd responded shockingly to his skillful lovemaking.

Now that she was thinking more clearly, she knew that letting herself fall into that sensual trap was wrong.

The worst part was it had suddenly become impossible to imagine a future without Shane Peters. Even when she knew there could be no future for the two of them. None.

No matter what she was feeling now or what she might feel later, she had to go back to her real life—her life in Beau Pays. Which meant she had to back away from Shane. And she had to find a way to apologize for leading him on.

Before she could dredge up the words she needed to say, they both heard a noise somewhere outside the room.

IN THE DIM LIGHT, SHANE THRUST Ariana behind him.

"What's that?" she whispered, her features tense.

His voice was low and even. "I don't know for sure. But I think we have to assume the guy who was shooting at us thinks we're down here."

She made a small sound. "What should we do?"

"Give him a surprise," Shane answered. Swiftly he bent to rummage in one of the boxes of clothing and other items that had been donated by church members.

As he dug through the contents, he silently cursed his behavior. Apparently, when he was around Ariana LeBron, he couldn't think straight. Once again, he'd gotten so wrapped up in her that he'd forgotten what he was supposed to be doing.

He'd been playing sex games with the princess. And someone out in the hall could be sneaking up to finish them off.

He found what he was looking for and wrapped the items in a couple of T-shirts. Then he transferred the sapphire to his jeans pocket.

Knowing that speed was important now, he scooped up the poles he'd taken from the rack. "Come on."

"Where?"

He managed not to answer with a curse. He wished he had a map of the church basement. Then he might have a better idea where to hide. But he knew one thing. If they stayed in this glass-walled room, they'd be trapped.

Quickly he ushered her toward the front of the church, toward a hallway that ran perpendicular to the one they were in. Mentally flipping a coin, he picked the left-hand branch.

"This way," he told Ariana, sending her ahead of him.

When they turned the corner, the stone wall shielded them from the previous corridor.

Shane hoped they could play hide-and-seek until he got his makeshift weapon ready. Opening another one of the meeting rooms, he pulled out two chairs, lining them up facing each other with their backs against the walls, then he laid the poles across the chair seats, creating a barrier that he hoped the gunman wouldn't see in the dim light.

Apparently they'd made it out of the little room just in time. Footsteps came toward them, slowly, stealthily, then stopped at the corner of the hallway.

Working with grim haste, Shane began getting his makeshift weapons ready. First he opened the can of shoe polish he'd taken from the box of clothing and household items. Then he began smearing the petroleum-based product on one of the T-shirts he'd also taken.

Of course, the guy around the corner could be some random Boston citizen who'd taken advantage of the blackout to come down here and look around for stuff to steal, but Shane didn't think so. Not when there were far more valuable treasures upstairs in the main sanctuary.

Unbidden, an unsettling thought leaped into his mind. When they'd been trying to escape from the gunman outside, FBI Agent Ben Parker had been drawn to the gunfire. And he'd given what sounded like a plausible reason for sending them into the church rather than back to the Hancock Tower, which had been swarming with cops and Secret Service agents.

In retrospect, that seemed like a bad decision.

Had the FBI agent innocently directed them into a trap? Or had he known exactly what he was doing?

What if the agent was one of the key players in the evening's plans? Maybe Liam Shea had paid him to help set up the hostage situation then pretend to guard the perimeter of Copley Square. What if Parker was really keeping people in the square rather than keeping people out?

As Shane sent his mind scrambling back over the evening, he couldn't remember seeing Parker during the crisis.

He hated to think the worst of the FBI agent. And he didn't know why the man would have been working with Liam Shea, since he didn't have any part in the original drama. But what if he'd needed money, and Shea had offered it to him?

Shane clenched his teeth. He didn't have time for a lot of speculation about Parker now. He'd better focus on the man coming down the hallway. At least it sounded as if there was only one other person out there. But what if Parker had come along to help take them down? What if he'd circled around the other way and now they were boxed in?

A voice rang out in the cavern of the church basement. "I've got you trapped, Peters. So give up."

He didn't bother to answer.

After a few seconds, the voice called out again, "Come out of hiding and I'll do you a favor."

Oh yeah?

"I'll shoot you first. Then you won't have to watch King Frederick's precious daughter die."

Beside him, Ariana suppressed a strangled sound.

He slid his arm around her, holding her close, trying to reassure her.

In the darkness, she brought her mouth close to his ear so she could speak without being heard. "That was pretty direct," she whispered.

"Yeah."

Still in a whisper, she continued, "He didn't have to call out to warn you he's coming. I think he wants to talk to you. Play with you for his own satisfaction. It sounds like you're right about who's behind the hostage situation."

He nodded against her lips.

"That means you can keep him busy talking while I look for a back way out."

He wanted to tell her it was too dangerous. Instead he said, "If you find another way out of the building, take it."

She sucked in a sharp breath as she absorbed the implication of what he was saying. "I'll come back for you."

"Get out while the getting's good," he ordered. "And don't come back."

Chapter Eleven

To Shane's relief, Ariana didn't stay around to argue. Instead she slipped into the darkness, and he was left to face the man who had already tried to kill them once.

"Who are you?" he called out.

Their nemesis answered with a harsh laugh. "Oh come on. I believe you can figure it out. Unless you're a lot stupider than I thought."

"I know you're one of the Sheas. But not Liam. And I know you let the president go but you still have Vice President Davis. So I've got to assume Liam is with him."

"Right. The vice president is the big prize!"

The man hadn't exactly answered the question, but the exchange gave Shane important information. Shea was just around the corner in the hallway. And he was sure Shane Peters didn't have a weapon, otherwise, he'd be making himself too much of a target.

To reinforce that conclusion, the man chuckled again. Apparently he figured he was in the catbird seat, and he was enjoying this game very much.

"Help me out here," Shane said, working to keep his voice conversational when he felt as if his throat was about to close. "I can understand that your old man is bitter. I can understand why he'd be crazy enough to take a roomful of high-profile hostages and start killing them. But you have your whole life ahead of you. Why are you throwing your future away?"

"I'm not!" The denial was followed by a string of curses that Shane hoped Ariana couldn't hear.

As he listened to the outburst, Shane decided she was right about this guy. He could have cut the conversation off by leaping around the corner with his gun blaring. Apparently he was as interested in talk as action.

That made him vulnerable. More importantly, the longer Shane kept the dialogue going, the more time Ariana had to get away. "Explain it to me, then," he said, as if he had all the time in the world to chat.

ARIANA RAN DOWN THE HALLWAY, working her way quietly toward the side of the church away from the Hancock Tower. Or at least she thought that was where she was going. In the darkness of the basement, she could be completely turned around.

But she did know one thing. Shane was doing his best to keep the man with the gun busy. And she would do her best to find a way out of here.

What if there wasn't an exit up this way? Then the guy with the gun had them trapped. Or worse, what if the man rushed Shane and started shooting? She didn't want to think about such an attack or what else might happen in this tomb-like basement. To Shane or to herself.

She'd told herself that she and Shane Peters didn't belong together. But that didn't stop her from caring about what happened to him.

When he'd dropped the sapphire, her fury at his duplicity had blazed up. Fury at him and fury at herself for letting him make a fool of her.

Maybe she should hold on to that anger and redirect it toward the gunman. Maybe that was the way to stay strong. She didn't know. Her emotions were too raw, so she tried to focus on the job she'd set herself as she moved as far away from the men as she could. But their voices still drifted toward her, and she found herself listening intently as she crept through the basement corridors.

It was obvious that the man out there hated Shane. She hoped Shane could use that knowledge to his advantage.

"I DIDN'T COME HERE TO TALK about myself," the man stalking them said. "I came to talk about you. I thought you were reasonably intelligent. What are you doing down here in this basement where you're trapped like a rat in a sewer?"

Shane didn't answer immediately. He knew there were at least two ways out of here—both on the wrong side of the gunman. Maybe Ariana would find another one that they could use.

"Well?" his tormentor demanded.

What answer would work best? What would keep this guy talking long enough for Ariana to get away?

Shane wound the shoe polish-smeared T-shirt around the can of pork and beans he'd picked up. And tied it to keep the can inside.

At the same time, he was mindful that he had to keep the conversation going, so he called out, "I'm down here because it seemed like the best way to keep Princess Ariana LeBron safe."

The man snorted. "Keep her safe. Oh sure. You brought her down here so you could be alone with her. I heard what you were doing. Taking advantage of her."

Shane felt his blood pressure shoot up. But he knew the taunt was designed to make him lose his cool and do something stupid—like maybe rush out into the open where the guy could shoot at him. Calmly he kept working on his weapon.

The man around the corner in the hallway raised his voice. Or maybe he'd used their conversation as a cover to get closer. "You couldn't even take care of your little brother. Why do you think you can take care of the princess?"

"Leave my brother out of this!" Shane growled.

"He was just a kid. You left him in foster care and went off to college."

Shane felt his stomach muscles clench. He was on the edge of losing his cool, but he knew that was what this guy wanted.

So he stuck with his original plan—keeping this guy engaged so Ariana could get away.

But he couldn't stop himself from thinking back over the choices he'd made in his life. His decision to get an education still haunted him. But he'd known that without a college degree, he was going to end up like his old man—with no skills and no way to get a good job. So he'd taken the full scholarship that MIT had offered him and gone off to school.

"I was just a kid, too," he shouted, hating the defensive sound of his answer.

"You were old enough to know what you were doing. Like your low-life father."

The jab hit home, and Shane could feel his blood

boiling. But he knew that losing his temper would be fatal. So he ordered himself to answer in an even voice. "I'm not my father."

"We all carry around the baggage our parents laid on us."

"You're speaking from personal experience?" Shane asked, regaining his calm. "You had some problems with your own father? Like when he went to prison and left your poor old mother to support her three sons."

The man didn't answer in words, but Shane heard him make an angry sound before starting to hurl insults again. "My father didn't have a choice. Your father slunk away into the night and left your mother flat. That was *his* decision. Nobody snatched him away from you."

Shane bit back a retort because anything insulting he said was going to inflame Liam Shea's son. Instead he started working on his second smoke bomb.

"Then *your* mom had to go out and take any menial job she could find," Shea called out.

"My mother did honorable work. What did you do— make a life study of my family?"

Shea snorted. "Of course. It's always best to know the enemy. I know about you and Chase and—" He stopped short.

"And who else?"

"We're talking about *you.* You grew up dirt poor. Is that why you have such a fancy house now? Is it why you only take on rich clients who can pay through the nose?"

"I do pro bono work," Shane answered, wishing he didn't feel the need to justify himself to this guy. Or was it Liam Shea's son he cared about?

He knew Ariana had to be listening because he could hear his voice echoing through the church basement. Maybe his answers were as much for her as they were for the man who taunted him.

As if Shea was picking up on his thoughts, he asked, "How do you like the princess hearing all this dirt about your family?"

"Keep her out of this!"

"Why? I came down here to kill her."

"Then you're wasting your time."

"I don't think so."

ARIANA CLENCHED HER HANDS into fists. The conversation had circled back to her again. To her death.

Determined to spoil the gunman's plans, she kept running. When she came to a place where another hallway branched off, she paused, then took a corridor lined with glass panels. To her relief, it led to a stairway. At the top was another hallway. This one led to what looked like office space. Beyond that was an exterior door. Hallelujah.

But when she got a little closer, she saw a sign that said Alarm Will Sound If Door Is Opened.

She wanted to scream in frustration. She had intended to open the door and prop it open with something heavy.

Change of plans. She couldn't take a chance that the alarm would sound—even with the power off.

Time to start back and tell Shane she'd found an exit.

Or she could still leave. Shane had told her to do that. And if she escaped from the church, she might find help outside. Maybe she'd even find that FBI agent again and tell him that Shane was in trouble.

Stopping in the darkness, she debated her best course of action. She could go for help, but by the time she brought anyone back, it might be too late. And she wasn't sure she trusted the agent who had sent her and Shane in here. He'd said they'd be safe in the church, but the man chasing them had found them.

In the darkness Shane got ready to make his move. The voice taunting him drew closer. *Come on, you bastard. Get yourself into a better position. Just a little closer,* he silently urged.

"What did I do to you?" he shouted.

"You know damn well what you did. Eleven years ago. And tonight. You stole that sapphire tonight, didn't you?"

"What's the sapphire to you?"

"I want it!"

"Well, I don't have it."

"You're a lying bastard. Do you like adding lying to your list of sins? Your dad went to jail for theft, didn't he? Was that your biggest aspiration—to end up like him?"

"Shut up," Shane snarled. He didn't have to listen to this. He could—

He could what?

He knew this guy was trying to push him into making a mistake. But he was too smart for that. He hoped.

"You think you've got tonight figured out," Shea shouted into the darkness. "You came up with the brilliant idea to steal the sapphire. But how do you think you found out that tempting green jewel was going to be at the reception, Mr. Genius Security Expert?"

"I…" Shane stopped. He'd gotten an e-mail that supposedly came from Ty. His friend had told him that the sapphire was going to be at the party. At the time, he hadn't questioned where the message had come from.

"That e-mail wasn't from your good friend Ty Jones. It was from us. We told you," the gunman bragged. "To make sure you showed up."

"Nice of you," Shane muttered. So he'd been suckered. But that didn't change anything now, he thought as he fumbled with the other item he'd found tucked into a shirt pocket in the charity collection. A box of matches.

Under the circumstances, they were priceless.

He pulled one out, holding it against the striking strip on the side of the box.

Almost time to spring his surprise.

Just before he could light the match, a flash of movement to his right made him whip his head around, prepared to fling the can without lighting the match.

When he saw it was Ariana coming toward him along the hallway, he clenched his teeth.

He'd told her to get out of here. And now she was back.

But why was he surprised? He already knew she was too stubborn to follow orders.

"I told you to leave."

"Not without you," she answered, speaking in a barely audible voice. "I found an exit. But we can't open it until we're both there. It says an alarm will sound."

"Go on. Get moving. Go back there and open the door."

"It will make noise."

"That's okay."

"I'm not going without you," she said again, and he detected that royal petulance in her voice. Too bad she'd been raised to expect lesser mortals to obey her.

He heaved in a breath and let it out. "You have to give me a little lead time. Go on. I'll be right behind you."

"Are you lying?"

"No," he answered, hoping that was the truth. He'd try to get to the door, but he didn't know if he could make it.

"Okay," she told him. Then just as she moved again, a bullet slammed against one of the walls of the hallway, making a resounding racket, and he knew he was out of time. The guy was moving in for the kill.

"Go," he ordered.

Apparently the bullet convinced Ariana it was time to split. She darted back the way she'd come, and he took several steps back along the corridor, pulling open one of the doors and using it as a shield while he scraped the match against the striker.

It was old and brittle and broke in his hand. Cursing, he had to start again, fumbling for another match out of the box.

This time he held it farther down the wooden shaft and worked more carefully, risking burning his fingers. To his relief, the head sputtered and ignited, and he quickly moved his fingers away from the flame.

He held the match to the T-shirt and the soft fabric flared up. Then the shoe polish on the cloth caught fire.

Black smoke suddenly billowed up from his makeshift smoke bomb, and he started to cough.

Another bullet hit nearby. Shane turned to face the end of the hallway, then threw the weighted T-shirt. It flew through the air and hit the stone floor.

"What the hell?" a man's voice rang out. The question was followed by coughing.

Good. Unfortunately, Shane was coughing, too.

He'd known the fumes from the burning shoe polish would be bad, but he hadn't known they would get to him so quickly.

Running feet pounded toward him along the hallway. They were followed by a loud clattering sound as the assailant rammed into the poles that Shane had stretched across the hallway between two chairs, and went sprawling on the hallway floor.

The clatter of the wood hitting the stone surface was accompanied by gritty curses.

"Now, now," Shane called as he sprinted down the hallway. "You don't want to defile a house of worship."

His only answer was more curses as the guy picked himself up. Maybe he'd sprained his knee or something.

At any rate, the poles had slowed Shea down. He was moving more slowly through the smoke, looking for more booby traps.

Shane took the opportunity to ready the second smoke bomb, but his hand wasn't quite steady as he lit another match and held it to the second T-shirt. Farther back in the hallway, he could hear the man's lungs continuing to protest, just as a loud ringing noise split the air.

The fire alarm. Thank God. He didn't want to damage one of Boston's landmarks. He only wanted to get away with his life.

When he found out how much the repairs cost, he'd send the church a check.

The sound of the other man's coughing receded, and Shane knew the smoke bomb had had the desired effect. Rather than shooting, Shea was thinking about how to save his own ass.

But in the billowing smoke, Shane was coughing, too. He wanted to turn and run. Before he lit out of there, he threw the other T-shirt-wrapped can onto the stone floor.

As HE BACKED AWAY from the smoke bomb, Colin shouted another curse.

Secretly he knew he'd waited too long, taunting that bastard Peters and giving him the time he needed to make his smoke bomb. But he'd never admit that out loud.

He longed to ignore his own coughing and leap into the billowing smoke so he could shoot down Peters and the princess. But now the fire alarm was ringing, and that would bring people running to save the old church.

He had to get away before the cavalry arrived and found him down here with a gun.

Bent low, he moved backward, hoping he was going in the right direction. The smoke was blinding and disorienting, and he had to give Peters credit for clever planning. Obviously, he'd thought of the smoke bomb and the poles a while ago, and he'd been working on it while they'd been having their heart-to-heart chat.

Colin cursed Shane and cursed his own gullibility. He'd thought he was in charge, but he'd been mistaken. And now he had to make sure he didn't pass out before he escaped from the church basement.

When he found the stairs he'd come down, he breathed out a sigh, the action causing another spasm in his chest. Still, he forced himself to keep moving, staggering upward into blessedly clean air.

In the darkness below, he could still hear coughing. Maybe Peters had trapped himself and the princess. Maybe the two of them would choke to death down there. Which would save him the trouble of hunting for them.

But he couldn't take anything for granted. Should he stay at the top of the stairs in case they came staggering up? Or should he go around the side of the building and look for another exit?

The sound of fire engines in the distance made up his mind. He didn't think the alarm would automatically go to the station in a blackout. But it looked as if some concerned citizen had alerted the authorities.

He staggered toward the door where he'd come in, anxious to get away before the firemen came. It was tough going because he felt as if he was breathing ground glass.

STILL COUGHING, SHANE RAN from the smoke.

He thought he knew which hallway to take. But when he came to two alternative routes, he stopped.

The smoke billowed behind him, filling his lungs, making his eyes water and choking off his thoughts. He could only hope the man with the gun was as blind and breathless as he was himself.

Up on the street, he heard the sound of fire engines. Or was that just the ringing in his own ears?

He wanted to sit down or crawl. Wouldn't the smoke be thinner near the floor?

He was about to lower himself to his hands and knees when someone grabbed his arm, and he tried to jerk away.

"It's me," Ariana whispered. "Let me show you where to find the stairs."

He straightened. Still coughing, he followed her down what felt like an endless passageway. Damn, he'd thought the smoke bomb was a great idea. Now he was beginning to question his own sanity.

He staggered up a flight of stairs, then down another hallway with a high counter to one side. When they got to the door, he stopped short.

"You didn't open it," he said as he stared at the wooden slab that blocked their exit.

Chapter Twelve

Shane closed his eyes, trying to center his thoughts.

Now what? Smoke was billowing after them, rising up the stairway and down the corridor, choking off their breath as Ariana tried but couldn't open the door.

In his present shape, could he? And what were their chances of running back the other way? Not good. Either the gunman was waiting for them or they'd be overcome by the smoke.

"It has one of those bars," she said, her words sputtering out between coughs, and he knew he had to get her out of this death trap that he'd created.

"We have to get down on the floor where the air is better," he managed to say.

They both sat down on the stone floor, and he rested his head against the cool wooden surface of the door. Just for a minute. It felt good. If he'd been alone, he might have just stayed there resting. But he was with Ariana and he had to take care of her. "Can you show me the knob?"

Her voice came out high and anxious. "I said it has a bar."

"A bar, yeah." He shook his head, trying to clear the

smoke from his brain. He felt as if his mind was shutting down.

In the thickening atmosphere, she groped for his hand, squeezed his fingers, then lifted his arm until he felt a metal bar that spanned the width of the door.

"Thanks," he croaked.

To give himself leverage, he got up on his knees and pushed on the bar. Nothing happened.

Repressing a curse, he brought all his weight down on the bar—and felt it give a little. Too bad the church caretaker hadn't oiled it recently.

"Help me," he gasped out. His lungs were so clogged that he could barely dredge up the breath to speak.

Ariana came up on her knees beside him and lent her weight to his, and they both pushed on the bar. With a screech of protesting metal, the locking device flew downward, sending them both falling out the door and onto a stone porch at the side of the church.

Shane looked behind him. He saw smoke but no flames, thank God.

He dragged in lungfuls of the fresh air, allowing himself a few seconds to rest before staggering to his feet and leaning against a stone pillar. "We have to get out of here. In case he comes around the church looking for us."

She glanced quickly toward the front of the church, then back to him. "Okay."

When he tried to climb down the short flight of stairs to street level, he could barely stay on his feet.

Ariana moved in close and held him up, and they staggered onto the sidewalk.

He knew they were on Boylston Street. The next block was Newbury Street, with its old town houses that had been converted to shops and restaurants.

He could hear the sound of breaking glass coming from the shopping district and knew that looters were still attacking the stores. Better to head into the nearby residential neighborhood where there should be fewer looters and other people crazy enough to be out here.

As he staggered along the sidewalk, her hand tightened on his arm. "You have to rest."

"Not…safe…yet," he said between panting breaths. His chest ached, but he ignored the pain and kept going.

Together they made it to the corner, then across the street, where they stopped short when they heard gunfire.

"That's him!" Ariana gasped.

"More likely…someone taking advantage of the blackout," he answered, leading her away from the church and toward the turn-of-the-century town houses and apartment buildings that lined the streets. They all backed onto narrow alleys, and he paused before plunging into one.

Looking behind them, he thought he saw a man hurrying toward the alley and pulled Ariana into the shadows of a Dumpster. As they pressed against the brick wall, a large rat scurried out from under the Dumpster and waddled for cover on the other side of the alley.

Ariana made a muffled sound, but Shane gave her credit for not screaming.

He risked a look around the side of the building but saw no one. Still, the guy could have kept up his hunt for the security expert and the princess. And he'd be angry that they'd escaped from the church basement.

Shane figured their best chance was to lose themselves in the city. He waited two minutes, then led

Ariana into the street, down the block and into another alley.

They were moving pretty fast, and the urge to cough tortured his throat and lungs. Since the sound would give them away, he ruthlessly kept himself from making any noise until they were another block from the church.

Doubling over, he began to hack. Once he'd started, he couldn't stop. Worse, he suddenly couldn't stand.

When he went down heavily on the brick pavement, Ariana crouched beside him.

"Shane!"

"I'll be okay."

"You can't keep going."

It was fruitless to argue the point. Somehow he pushed himself to his feet. But as he staggered along, he stopped often, feeling along the underside of the vehicles they passed.

"What are you doing?"

"Taking advantage of stupidity," he answered.

After a few cars, he found what he was looking for—a key attached to the underside of the chassis with a magnet.

Leaning against the side of the car, he tried to insert the key in the lock. It took several tries before he was coordinated enough to do it.

"Where did you get that?" Ariana gasped out.

"Under the car. A lot of motorists leave them."

She stared at the vehicle, which had to be at least fifteen years old.

"What's a car like this doing in a…swanky neighborhood?"

"Maybe it belongs to a cook."

She nodded and climbed into the passenger side.

Sliding behind the wheel, he allowed himself to rest for a moment. He wouldn't have tried to drive on the freeway in his present condition, but he knew that getting them away from the church was their best chance of staying alive. So he cranked the engine, then promptly started coughing.

"Move over," Ariana said.

"You have…a driver's license?" he asked between coughs.

"No. But I know how to drive. And what does a license matter when the car is stolen?"

"Borrowed! We'll leave it where the cops can find it."

"A technicality. Move."

He wasn't accustomed to taking orders from a princess. But he'd already found out that she was used to giving them. Because he didn't want to put up the effort to fight her, he climbed out. When he stood again, he found his legs were shaky, and he silently admitted that the smoke had done a number on him. He hoped the other guy was in worse shape.

When he was settled in the passenger seat, Ariana started the engine and drove away. It was hot in the car, and the air-conditioning didn't seem to be working. So she rolled down the windows.

"Drive slowly. Keep your lights off until we get out of the area, and keep an eye out for pedestrians."

"Okay."

As she crept along the deserted street, he added, "See if you can find a place with low trees, where it will be hard to see if someone's in the car."

She kept driving, but the houses were too densely packed together to allow for many trees. In this neighborhood, the structures all looked to be about a hundred years old, with stone facades, bay windows, steep roofs and other architectural details popular at the turn of the century.

Finally, when she came to a parking place in front of a large stone mansion, he said, "I guess this will have to do."

She pulled into the space, and he sat with his head thrown back against the headrest.

BACK AT THE HANCOCK TOWER, Special Agent Harold Wolf of the FBI was in charge of the mop-up operation. He was working out of the security desk in the building's lobby, though he would rather have been out looking for Vice President Grant Davis, who was still missing.

At this point, official information on the incident in the tower was still sketchy. Nobody knew how the bad guys had crashed the party, nor how they had gotten Vice President Davis out of the building. They could still be in there, hiding in one of the offices, for all Wolf knew. But if they were, the agents combing the tower from top to bottom would find him.

So far there was no word on that. But at least something was going right. President Stack was at a secure location outside the city, and about half the guests who had been held captive in the top-floor reception room had been taken out of the area.

Those who lived nearby wanted transportation home. Others had come from out of town and wanted to be driven to their hotels so they could pick up their luggage before leaving the city. For the moment, none of them were going anywhere besides Otis Air Force Base on

Cape Cod, where they could be debriefed. And also where the Bureau could determine if any of them had been in on the takeover of the building.

Wolf craned his neck toward the front of the building. Media trucks were still parked out on the street. Too bad they couldn't keep the whole incident quiet. But this was the age of instant media attention. Despite tight security, the hostage situation and its resolution had hit the networks. Including *CNN,* which broadcasts not only in the U.S. but around the world.

No sooner had the thought surfaced than a young Secret Service agent came running up.

"We have a call from King Frederick of Beau Pays," the man said. From the sound of his voice, it wasn't a "thank you for saving my daughter" call.

"The princess was one of the guests upstairs, and he wants to know if she's okay. He's holding on one of the temporary lines."

"Tell him everything's fine. We have the situation under control," Wolf said, giving his standard answer.

The man cleared his throat. "There may be a glitch as far as his daughter is concerned."

Wolf raised his head from the clipboard he was holding. "Oh yeah?"

The man consulted his own notes. "She came downstairs with a guy from a private security company who happened to be at the reception. Then she was supposed to be sent out on one of the first helicopters."

"And?"

"She's not on the list of people who arrived at Otis. When she didn't show up, we started checking around. FBI Agent Parker saw her run from the helicopter. Her and the security guy."

"Why the hell would she do that?"

"She told him someone was shooting at her."

Wolf felt his stomach muscles clench. Just what he needed. A missing princess from a small European country. "Where the hell is she?"

The agent shrugged. "Lost? Kidnapped? What should I tell King Frederick?"

"Don't tell him his daughter is missing. Tell him we're trying to ascertain her whereabouts. Then find out where the hell she went—and if she's still with the security guy." He thought for a moment, then added, "And alert the Boston police. Maybe that will do us some good."

The agent was still standing there.

"What?" Wolf asked.

"The king also mentioned a jewel. The Beau Pays sapphire. It was on display at the reception."

"What about it?"

"The king wants to know if it's safe."

"I guess you'd better send someone up there to look," Wolf suggested.

"Okeydoke."

The man hurried off, probably wishing that someone else had caught the call from the ruler of Beau Pays.

WHEN ARIANA CUT THE ENGINE, Shane sat with his head thrown back and his eyes closed. He was still coughing occasionally, but the spasms were less often and less intense than they had been a few minutes ago.

Ariana shifted, and his eyes blinked open to find her leaning over him, looking worried.

"You should go to a hospital."

"I don't think so."

"You're not too macho to get checked out, are you?"

He gave a little shake of his head. "In the middle of a blackout every hospital in the city will be a zoo. There will be people with heart attacks. People in automobile accidents. People who need emergency surgery. All of them will need the attention of the medical staff a lot more than I do."

She sighed. "Okay."

"You're not going to argue?" he muttered.

She made a small sound. "I've found that arguing with you doesn't get me very far."

"Funny, I have the same experience with you."

She didn't offer a comeback, so he sat with his eyes closed for several moments, until she cleared her throat.

"Can I ask you a question?" she murmured.

"You're going to do it anyway, right?"

"When that guy was talking about your brother, he meant…"

"Chase," Shane supplied. "My half brother, actually."

"How did he know about Chase?"

"Apparently the Sheas studied my background. They know that my dad went to prison when I was little. Mom divorced him and married Mr. Vickers. He got her pregnant with Chase, then got himself run over."

"And your mom had to support the two of you."

"Yes. I guess you could say she worked herself to death trying to provide for us." Before she could offer any sympathy, he went on quickly. "And I abandoned Chase when he was a little kid."

"How old were you?"

"Eighteen."

"What was your alternative? Working at a fast-food restaurant so you could support the two of you on a poverty income?"

He stared straight ahead through the windshield into the darkness beyond. "I had good grades. With my non-existent income, it wasn't so hard to get a scholarship to MIT. I left Chase in foster care so I could go to school."

"Leaving him must have been a hard decision," she said softly.

"Yeah. I've always felt guilty about it."

"But you could see how hard it was for your mom to make ends meet. I guess that's why you knew that a college education would give you a better chance."

"Yeah. She worked as a hotel maid. It didn't pay well, but it was a steady job. So I didn't grow up in cir-cumstances anything like yours," he added, just to make that clear.

"Are you ashamed of your background?" she asked in a soft voice.

"Should I be?"

"You should be proud of how well you've done. You're a self-made man." She turned toward him in the dark. "And I'll bet you give money to a lot of charities for disadvantaged children."

He made a strangled sound. "How do you know?"

"Because you know how hard it is to grow up poor, and you're trying to give those kids a better chance."

He felt her studying him in the darkness.

"You give your money," she murmured. "You give your time, too. You're a…what do they call it? A Big Brother, too."

"Yeah." He was embarrassed, but he needed to add, "I believe that the right role models can make up for an awful lot of other sins."

"You overcame a difficult background."

"I stole your sapphire," he heard himself saying and wished he wasn't bent on making sure Princess Ariana backed off.

Instead, she absolved him. "I understand why. I don't like it, but I understand."

"I'm not proud of doing it," he admitted. "In retrospect, it was a dumb idea."

He heard her swallow in the darkness. "You don't have a monopoly on that. When I was angry with you out in Copley Square, I could have gotten us both killed."

"Well, as you said a moment ago, I understand why you were angry." He wanted to reach out and clasp her hand, but he didn't allow himself that luxury. Touching her was not a great idea, because if he put his hand on hers, he would want to do a whole lot more.

Maybe the conversation was getting too personal for her, too, because she switched the subject.

"If I had to guess, I'd say Liam Shea brainwashed his sons into going along on his hostage-taking scheme."

Glad that she'd focused on the enemy, he answered, "I was thinking the same thing."

In the darkness, she dragged in a breath and let it out in a rush. "Something else I've been thinking. If tonight was so important to Liam Shea, I'm guessing that he really was innocent of the charges."

Shane nodded. "Which means one of the team members set him up. And maybe he thinks he can get that man to confess before he kills him."

"Charming." She made a small sound. "It wasn't my father!"

"I didn't think so."

"And it wasn't you!"

"How do you know? Maybe a man who would steal a sapphire would betray his team members." He wasn't sure why he'd said that. Perhaps because he wanted to hear her come to his defense.

"We both know you didn't do it. And you don't have to bring up that chunk of rock again."

"Don't call it a chunk of rock. It's been important to your family for generations."

She pressed her finger to his lips. "Let's not talk about it again, okay?"

He nodded, and she stroked her fingers against his lips. It wasn't what he'd expected, and he felt instant arousal shoot through him.

He'd promised himself he wouldn't touch her. But she was the one who had initiated the contact. He thanked fate for giving him a little longer with her, and he ached to take advantage of this time. But he'd already made enough mistakes with her. To keep from doing anything else he'd regret, he opened the door and climbed out of the car.

Ariana did the same, coming around to his side of the vehicle but standing several feet away from him.

She scuffed her foot against the pavement, then looked over at him. "So who framed Liam Shea? And why?"

"It wasn't any of the guys I've kept in close contact with. Not Chase. Not Ethan Matalon—who wasn't here tonight. And not Ty Jones, the Secret Service agent."

"Two other men were on the mission besides my father, right?"

"Yes. The commander of the team, Tom Bradley, is dead. But I thought he was an honorable man."

"Like Brutus?"

Shane dealt with another fit of coughing, then said, "You mean in *Julius Caesar?* Brutus helped assassinate Caesar because he thought he was taking down a tyrant?"

She nodded.

"I don't think that's the case here. Bradley testified against Shea. But I don't think he would have set him up."

She turned to face him. "That leaves one more man who went along on the mission."

"The vice president."

"What do you know about him?"

"Not much."

"Would he have set himself up as a war hero to advance his career?"

Shane felt a wave of sickness in his throat. "I hope not. It's hard to view him in that light."

She looked toward the nearest town houses, then back at him. "Tell me some more about the mission."

"You don't really want to hear any more of the gory details."

"Maybe I can help you figure out what happened."

He sighed. "The court reviewed the evidence and convicted Shea."

"But now we have new information, if we can determine what's relevant."

"Yeah."

"You said Shea cut the power to the building too soon, which alerted the hostage takers that you were coming in to free the prisoners. But why would he do that? He didn't want the team to fail, did he?"

Shane thought about that long-ago night and the trial afterward.

"Shea said somebody gave him the signal to go ahead. But he didn't have any proof, and the court put it down to his error. The failure was judged to be his fault."

"He was wounded, right?"

"How do you know?"

"When my father wouldn't talk about it, I looked up accounts of the mission. But I never got all the details."

Before he could fill in some of the blanks, the sound of footsteps made them both go rigid.

He wanted to shout at Ariana to get back in the car. But he knew it was already too late when shadowy figures came out of the darkness, boxing them in between the car and a brick wall.

Chapter Thirteen

Shane felt every muscle in his body tense.

"Put your hands up, or I'll slice your head off," a hard voice ordered.

Slice his head off? Like in one of those terrorist videos out there on the Internet? Was that where this thug was getting his lines?

Maybe. But the guy speaking looked and sounded more like a street punk than a terrorist. A street punk with a knife. Shane had always liked a good knife fight, although he wasn't exactly in great fighting shape at the moment. And he realized that the knife he'd had at the beginning of the evening was back in his tuxedo pocket.

Even in the dark he detected a flash of movement and flicked his eyes to the right, seeing another guy on the other side of Ariana.

Shane managed not to mutter a curse as he sized up the opposition, grateful that at least he'd gotten his breath back. Thank God, because it looked as if he didn't have much choice about defending himself and Ariana.

Beside him, she had gone rigid.

He kept his gaze away from her and studied the guy

nearest to him. The punk looked to be in his late teens or early twenties, with shoulder-length dark hair that was limp with grease, big prominent teeth and a little goatee that seemed completely out of place on his youthful face.

He held a hunting knife in his right hand. Probably the wide, slightly curved blade gave him a sense of invincibility. Shane hoped the guy was in for a shock.

"Bring the woman over here," he called out to his accomplice.

Shane felt his gut clench as the other assailant took a step toward Ariana. His hair was shorter than his friend's, and he was clean-shaven, but he had a safety pin piercing his left eyebrow. Like his partner he was dressed in faded jeans and a dark T-shirt. And he also carried a knife. Probably these hoods thought that the blackout was a good time to advance their fortunes, and they'd come across two honest citizens who should have stayed inside where they belonged.

Ariana looked terrified. He ached to tell her everything was going to be okay. At the same time, he wanted to shout out that if they did anything to hurt the woman, they were dead.

But he figured that in the present situation, surprise was his best ally. So he kept his mouth shut, his posture slightly slumped, and his gaze fixed on the two troublemakers as he considered his options.

The four of them were standing on the sidewalk in an upper-class Boston neighborhood.

He doubted any of the local residents would come running out of their houses if he shouted for help. The residents would be keeping their heads down, hoping to make it through the blackout in one piece.

"Give me your wallet," one of the punks demanded.

"I don't have one," Shane answered. He was telling the truth. His wallet was back at the church. Not that he would have given it up if he'd had it.

"Don't give me that crap."

"I came outside without it."

The thug gave Ariana an appraising look, then turned back to Shane. "She's a pretty little thing. Did you sneak out of the house to meet her in the car?"

"No," Shane clipped out.

"Let's see what you've got."

Swaggering a little now, the man moved in, then spotted the bulge in the front pocket of Shane's jeans. "What's that?"

"Nothing."

Only the Beau Pays sapphire.

When the man reached toward the pocket, Shane moved, slapping the hand away, and at the same time bringing his other hand up to deflect the knife that came slicing down toward his throat.

He'd had training in street-fighting methods, and even without a knife, he was better prepared to defend himself than the guy attacking him.

"Run," he yelled to Ariana as he lashed out at the man's knife arm.

To his dismay, she did just the opposite. As he moved forward, so did she. She kicked out at the man standing over her, catching him squarely in the crotch.

The man bellowed and doubled over, which gave Ariana the opportunity to bring her hand down in a chopping motion on his shoulders, just below his neck.

Shane noticed the move. Noticed, too, that she could have killed the guy if she'd moved her hand an inch higher. The action told him that she'd had very professional defensive training along with her art and dancing lessons.

That knowledge flashed through his mind as he fought with the other thug, moving his arms in rhythm to deflect the knife slashes, then catching the guy's elbow and thrusting the knife back toward him, so that the assailant cut his own shoulder.

He cried out in pain and surprise.

"Come on," Shane offered between pants. "You want some more punishment? I'll be glad to give it to you."

Both men cursed. The one who'd been chopped by Ariana scrambled to his feet and backed away, his friend following. When they were ten feet from Shane and Ariana, they turned and ran.

"Where did you learn those moves?" Shane asked, hoping he didn't sound like he needed a respirator.

Ariana gave him what she hoped was a cocky smile. "Part of my private lessons."

"The part you didn't mention." He laughed appreciatively. "Remind me not to get on your bad side."

As they stood there in the moonlight, she felt her whole body tingling. "That was quite exhilarating," she said. "I never thought I'd actually be in hand-to-hand combat."

"You are a very brave woman."

"I don't think I had a choice."

"Yeah." He dragged in a breath and let it out. "I want to ask you a question."

She nodded.

"A few minutes ago, you were fighting for your life. Back at the reception, you were going to turn yourself in. Did you think you could fight off men armed with automatic weapons?"

"No."

"So you were going to let them kill you?"

She gave him a direct look. "What would *you* have done if they'd said they'd start killing innocent people unless you turned over Shane Peters?"

She knew he'd taken the point when he winced, then said, "I would have had to go up there."

"Then you understand my dilemma."

"But your country needs you."

She folded her arms across her chest. "Sometimes rulers have to make hard choices."

He spoke to her the way her father might have spoken. "The hard choice may be keeping yourself safe so you can rule your country and continue the Beau Pays line."

"And live with the guilt of causing the deaths of innocent people?"

"Yes. That might be the kind of decision you have to make when you're sitting on the throne. It's like the president of the United States. They put him on a helicopter and got him out of Boston while everybody else had to wait."

"And before that he was willing to turn himself over to the gunmen to save people's lives."

He nodded, conceding the point.

She made a frustrated gesture with her arm. "Too bad I don't live a couple of hundred years ago when rulers could do anything they wanted."

"If they went too far, sometimes they got executed. You know, like Louis XVI. Or Charles I of England. Or several Russian czars I can think of."

"Thanks for reminding me."

He gave her a crooked grin. "It's easier to give advice when it doesn't apply directly to you."

"Let's not get too far off track," she said, reminding herself that she hadn't been planning to get into another fight with Shane Peters. Quite the contrary.

Deliberately, she looked around at the darkened houses on either side of the street.

She took a step toward the wall to their right, then made a small sound of pain when she put weight on her right ankle.

"What happened?" he asked.

"I must have twisted my ankle in the fight," she answered.

"And I was standing here arguing with you. You need to sit down."

"Yes."

She limped over to the wall, being careful not to put much weight on the foot. When she reached the vertical surface, she leaned against it.

"We just had a demonstration of how dangerous it is to be out here in the blackout," Shane said. "Maybe we should go back to your previous plan and head for the nearest police station."

"I can't walk very far. And we can't drive up to a police station in a stolen car," she murmured.

He looked back at the car they'd borrowed. "You have a good point there."

Surveying the darkened street, he said, "If we tried to walk, you could lean on me."

"But we'd have to go pretty slowly. And those men could come back. Or we could bump into someone else with robbery on their minds."

She moved along the wall, favoring her right foot, then stopped when she came to a wooden door. "Maybe this will open."

Before he could tell her it was a bad idea, she turned the handle and the door swung inward.

"We'll be safer inside than on the street. But not if someone sees us going in. Hurry," she said, moving inside as quickly as she dared.

Once inside, she held her breath until Shane followed. They were in a walled garden. The house must have been on a double lot because it was more than fifteen yards away. They were standing in a landscaped area that included a small swimming pool.

"So you're adding breaking and entering to car theft?" he asked, his voice teasing.

"Apparently." As she looked around their refuge, she leaned her hand against the back of a garden bench. When she saw the small building on the other side of the pool, she caught her breath.

"What?"

"The summerhouse."

"What about it?"

Her mouth was so dry that she could hardly speak. "I…imagined it. I mean I saw it in my mind. And here it is. The same place."

"You saw it? When?"

"Back at the reception, when we were under the control of the Sheas," she said in a low voice. "I wanted to escape to a place like that. And here it is."

She didn't add that it had been when they were under the table, when he'd been trying to take her mind off what was going on around them by kissing her.

"It must be a sign," she murmured. *A sign that I'm doing the right thing.* The thought lodged in her mind, but she didn't speak it aloud.

"A sign of what?"

"That we're supposed to be here," she said. Feeling vindicated, she limped farther into the garden and toward the summerhouse.

"You believe in signs and portents?"

"Well, I'd never admit to my father that I do. But there have been times in my life when they were important."

"Like when?"

"Like when I was a little girl, and I was afraid to go out on one of the balconies at home. I kept dreaming that it would fall off the castle. Then one night, in a big storm, it did."

"Coincidence."

"Well, I wasn't afraid of any of the other balconies. Just that one. So I don't think so."

"Do you need help walking?"

"No," she answered as she crossed the cement deck beside the pool.

"What if the home owner comes out with a shotgun?" he asked.

"They're not home."

"How do you know?"

"The lights are off," she answered, then started to giggle.

"The lights are off all over the city," he reminded her.

"That's why it's funny. But I think they would have heard the knife fight. Then they would have been listening and come out with big flashlights to challenge us when we came through the gate."

"What would you have done?"

She drew herself up taller. "I would have told them they were providing refuge to Princess Ariana of Beau Pays, and I would give them a reward in return." She looked back at him. "In case you can't tell, that's her royal highness talking."

"I can tell."

She opened the door to the summerhouse and said, "Do you still have those matches?"

"Yes."

"There are candles in here." She held up two glass jars that had been sitting on one of the low tables.

"Okay." He struck a match and lit the candles, then set them back on the tables. They cast a warm glow around the little room, flickering on the furniture and the man standing next to her.

SHANE COULDN'T TAKE HIS EYES off Ariana. She looked so beautiful that his throat tightened. It tightened even further when she sat down on what looked like a double bed but was probably a double-wide chaise longue with the backrest in the flat position. The chaise was set at an angle so that it took up the center of the room.

She reached to take off her shoes, then turned so she could swing her legs onto the cushion. After rolling up the leg of her jeans, she bent to assess the damage to her ankle, running her fingers from her foot to her calf. He assumed she was trying to see how badly she'd hurt herself, but the gesture came across as erotic. Seductive.

He stood by the table, staring down at the top of her blond head, thinking how much he'd love to run his hand over the same territory she'd traveled. Then he reminded himself that she was hurt.

"How bad is it?" he asked, hearing the thickness of his own voice.

"I don't know. Maybe you'd better check it out."

He crossed the sisal rug and sat down beside her on

the chaise, then circled her ankle with his fingers. Her bones were so delicate, her skin so smooth that he forgot for a minute what he was supposed to be doing. Even when he told himself the contact was entirely innocent, he couldn't prevent himself from getting aroused as he carefully probed the ankle.

"It feels okay," he finally said. "Maybe you can walk now."

He heard her swallow before she raised her head toward him. "It's fine. I told you I hurt it to get you in here."

He reared back. "What are you doing? It sounds like you're the one playing games."

"No."

When he started to stand, she grabbed his wrist.

"Maybe you'd better explain yourself," he ordered.

"I wanted to be alone with you," she answered.

"Not a good idea."

"What are you afraid of?"

He gave her a hard look. "Nothing. You're the one who should be worried."

She raised her chin defiantly and looked him in the eye. "I'm not afraid of you. I'm afraid of what I've turned into. A woman who is all about responsibilities. To my country. To my father. And there's nothing left over for myself."

"You have to find a balance."

Ignoring him, she went on, "I've always been a good little girl, doing everything I was supposed to do. Tonight, I want to escape from that. I want to be with you. We're a man and a woman who want to make love with each other. I don't want to walk away from that. I don't want to walk away from you."

Shane was still struggling with his own desires and reality. "You're going to have to walk away from me. After tonight, you won't see me again."

"I thought you wanted the contract for Beau Pays security."

In frustration, he ran a hand through his hair. "I did. But that was before I met you and we..."

"Developed a personal relationship?" she asked.

"Yes. Which means I can't accept a contract from your father now even if he offered it to me."

"Why not? You went to a lot of trouble to get it."

If she wanted him to spell it out, he would. "What would happen when I went to your country? We'd see each other, and we'd want each other. And you wouldn't cheat on your husband. Or at least, I don't think you're that kind of royal."

She ignored most of what he'd said and zeroed in on the basic issue. "You're admitting you want me?"

"You know I do," he answered.

"Well, I'm not married now."

"And you're supposed to be a virgin when you marry," he snapped back.

"But I'm making a different choice." She laughed. "One of the hard choices you told me a ruler has to make."

"What's your bridegroom going to do if he finds out you're not...untouched?"

"I'll tell him about it first. If he rejects me, I think there are other men who would apply for the job of consort."

"You'll tell him about us?"

"No, I'll tell him I have a past. But enough arguing. Do you really want to waste the time we have together?"

Leaning forward, she pressed her lips to his. Earlier, he might have had the strength to pull himself away, but he'd lost the will to deny her—or to deny himself what he wanted so badly. The pressure of her lips against his felt as if someone had completed an electric circuit. Current leaped back and forth between them, sparked around them, stole the breath from their lungs. When she raised her head, they were both gasping for air.

"It's like the smoke but a lot more potent," she whispered. "And a lot more pleasurable."

"You're forgetting a major problem. I have no way to protect you," he forced himself to say.

"From pregnancy?"

"Yeah."

"I think they've invented something called Plan B. I can take it tomorrow."

"And what about an STD?"

She gave him a direct look. "Are you telling me you have one?"

"No."

She smiled. "Thank God."

BACK AT THE HANCOCK TOWER, Special Agent Wolf was still on the scene, although it was long past time for his shift to end.

He kept hoping that someone would come running up and tell him they'd found Vice President Davis alive and well.

No such luck. And the same was true for the princess from Beau Pays.

When one of the Secret Service agents came dashing up, his expression was grave.

"Now what?" Wolf snapped.

"We got a police report that the princess may have been in a street fight."

"What?"

"A woman matching her description was spotted by a home owner in the Back Bay—in a fight with two punks and another man."

"She was fighting all three of them?"

"One of them seemed to be on her side. She and the guy fought the other two off."

"The informant watched all that and didn't go out to help?"

"He says he's in his eighties."

"Okay. Where is she now?"

"The old guy went to get his cell phone. When he came back, she'd vanished."

Wolf answered with a curse. "She couldn't have vanished, unless she's a witch as well as a princess. Maybe the man she was with abducted her. Do you have the street address?"

"Yes."

"She may not be the princess at all, but we have to find out. I want a team dispatched there. As soon as possible."

"We can't spare a team of Secret Service agents. And we can't send just one guy on his own."

Wolf controlled the urge to vent his frustration. He'd come up through the ranks, and he'd learned to hate supervisors who shot the messenger. "Ask the Boston PD to help us out."

"I can ask. But they have their hands full with incidents around the city. Traffic accidents. Robberies."

Wolf sighed. "Tell them we'd be extremely appreciative if they found the princess."

"It would help if we had a picture of her."

Wolf thought for a moment. He'd seen a picture. Now where the hell was it?

"There was a briefing folder on the guests attending the party." He started riffling through the papers spread across the desk at the security station. By some miracle he was able to put his hands on the folder. And when he pawed through the contents, he found a picture of her royal highness.

"Here," he said, handing over the photograph. "Take it to the watch commander at the closest police station to the location mentioned."

Chapter Fourteen

Shane watched Ariana shake her head. "Don't try to talk me out of this night with you because you think it's for my own good. Or are you saying you don't want me?"

He couldn't hold back a curse.

Helpless to hide his feelings, he gathered her close. Bringing his lips to hers, he ravaged her mouth, hungry for the taste of her, the texture of her lips, the sweetness of her.

She held on to him, her mouth fused to his, as she lay back, bringing him down to the horizontal surface of the chaise so that he was half-sprawled on top of her. She'd been bold with her verbal request. This was even more explicit.

Lifting his head, he looked down into her eyes, so large and luminous in the flickering light from the candles.

"You're awfully bold for a virgin princess," he murmured.

"What fun is being a princess if you can't issue commands?" She gave him a wicked grin. "Like…undress me." The statement and her expression were brazen, but he heard the quaver in her voice.

He knew she was fighting raw nerves. So was he. Making love with the heir to the throne of Beau Pays was more responsibility than he'd bargained for. Yet at the same time, he was awed. She was offering him a precious gift. A gift that he ached to accept. But with acceptance came responsibilities.

"I've read about how to do this," she said.

He grinned. "Oh yeah?"

"First you undress me. You arouse me by kissing me and touching me. My breasts. My… Between my legs. You make sure I'm wet and slippery so you know I'm ready for you. Then we have intercourse."

He made a strangled sound. "You're being pretty direct."

"I decided I have to be."

She reached for his hand and pressed it over her right breast. The warmth and softness of her was incredible. When he felt her hardened nipple stab into his palm, his own degree of arousal went up several notches on the hardness scale.

She was pushing him toward the edge of a precipice, and as he thought back over the past hour, he suspected she'd been planning her strategy since they'd been sitting in the car. If the two punks hadn't attacked them, what would she have done—pretended to trip so she could manufacture a twisted ankle?

"There's more to it than breasts and your…" He fumbled for a good word and came up with "Lady Jane."

She laughed softly. "Lady Jane? Is that what you Americans call it?"

"Sometimes," he answered. "When we don't want to come across as uncivilized in the eyes of European royalty."

"Never."

"Don't tell me you weren't thinking of me as an American upstart."

"Just at the beginning. But don't change the subject. Lady Jane is waiting for your attention." She kept her gaze on his face as she took his hand and moved it down her body, pressing it to the vee at the top of her legs, her breath hitching as she absorbed the caress.

He couldn't hold back a soft curse. "Too much too fast."

"I'm trying to make sure you don't chicken out."

"Nobody ever called me a chicken."

"Good."

She had told him very vividly what she wanted. And it was the same thing he wanted. Exactly the same.

Yet he knew her behavior was as much a charade as an act of boldness.

IN A SECRET LOCATION NEAR the Hancock Tower, Colin Shea clicked off his police scanner and called a special number on a secure cell phone.

"Are you all right?" one of his brothers asked.

"Yeah. And I know where to find the princess. I got the information off the police frequency," he said, his tone smug to hide the relief he was feeling. He'd lost her royal highness. Now he had her back again.

"Good going," his brother answered, and Colin was thankful that Finn didn't mention the previous screwup.

"She's still in the Back Bay. Some old guy saw her and a man—I assume it's Peters—in a fight with two street punks. Then he lost sight of her. But they can't get far."

"The trouble is, the FBI is sending the police to that location, so maybe I'd better get there first." Colin checked the clip on his Glock. He'd checked it before, after the fiasco at the church, but he was too nervous to trust his memory.

"Take one of the cars."

"I will. And I'll be back as soon as I kill her."

SHANE KEPT HIS GAZE ON ARIANA as he unbuttoned his shirt. When he'd tossed the garment aside, her expression was a good deal more tense.

"You've never been close to a naked man. Right?" he asked.

She swallowed. "No."

The edge of nerves in her voice told him he'd better keep his pants on for a while, even if the fabric stretched across his crotch was causing him pain.

As she had done earlier, he lifted her hand and brought it to his chest. She closed her eyes, moving her fingers against his skin and through the mat of hair she encountered there.

"But you've seen guys in bathing suits," he said. "What kind of chest do you like?"

"This kind," she said, stroking some more, then flattening her hand over the left side. "Your heart is pounding."

"Yeah."

"I like knowing that I can do that to you."

"My heart started pounding the moment I saw you."

"Mine, too," she whispered.

"Ariana." He breathed her name as he bent to stroke his lips against her jaw, then slid lower, caressing the elegant column of her neck with his tongue, nibbling with his teeth, pushing her shirt collar aside so he could feather kisses on her collarbone.

He wasn't modest about his lovemaking abilities. He knew he was good at pleasing his partners. But pleasing *this* woman had become the most important thing in the world.

As he nibbled at her silky skin, he opened the buttons down the front of her shirt, following the progress of his fingers with soft kisses. When he'd opened the shirt all the way down, he pushed back the fabric just enough so that he could press his lips to the side of one breast and then the other.

He heard her breath quicken, felt her stir restlessly against him. Smiling against her skin, he pushed the front panels of her shirt fully open, pausing to admire the treasure he'd uncovered before cupping her breasts, lifting them gently in his hands so that he could lightly kiss each coral nipple.

"Your breasts are so warm and soft. And so beautiful," he murmured.

"Are they?"

"They're perfect."

"I'm not…a *Playboy* centerfold."

"Right. You haven't spoiled them with a trip to the plastic surgeon."

Still smiling, he bent to kiss each inner curve, then turned his head so he could lick at one nipple.

"Oh! That's good."

"Very." He raised up enough to suck the nipple into his mouth, gratified by the way she arched into the caress. As he used his lips and tongue on her, he took the other nipple between his thumb and forefinger, plucking and twisting it, judging from her response how much stimulation she liked.

"I want to feel your chest against me," she whispered, sitting up and lifting her arms around his neck, pulling him close, then moving her breasts against him, the contact making him catch his breath.

"That's wonderful," she gasped.

"Over here, too."

He helped her pull her arms out of her sleeves, then tossed the shirt aside before laying her back down, so that he could kiss his way to the waistband of her jeans, where he opened the snap with his free hand and lowered the zipper.

As he watched her face, he eased his hand inside her panties, playing with the crinkly hair he encountered, then gliding lower to slip into her slick folds.

She made a low sound, lifting her hips toward his questing fingers, showing him with her little cries and sounds of approval what she liked best. Watching her face, he dipped his finger inside her, then slid it up to her most sensitive flesh.

"You're going to push me over the edge," she gasped, reaching down to still his hand.

He kissed her on the mouth, then because he wanted her busy while he pulled off his pants, he said, "Can you take your jeans off for me?"

They were both naked when he came down beside her on the mattress again, his erection pressed to her thigh.

"You're going to do it now?" she asked, her voice a little shaky.

"When you're ready."

"I am."

He grinned at her. "We'll see."

He began to kiss her again, her mouth, her shoulder, her breasts, while his hand found her center, teasing and stroking, and urging her upward until she was crying out for him to finish it.

He moved between her legs, his eyes on her face, and his throat tight. "I don't want to hurt you."

"Maybe you won't."

He entered her quickly, in one smooth stroke, his breath stopping as she cried out.

"Are you all right?" he whispered.

"I will be." She clasped her arms around his shoulders, holding him close. He kissed her cheek, her lips, keeping very still, then moving slowly, judging her reaction as he increased the pace. "Put your hands on your breasts. Play with your nipples," he murmured.

She looked shocked.

"I want to see that," he whispered because it was the truth and because he knew it would help tip the balance for her.

She did it, tentatively at first, and then gave herself over to the added pleasure.

Soon she was clutching his shoulders again, her hips rising and falling urgently in rhythm with his. He slipped his hand between them, pressing against the spot where he knew her orgasm centered.

She cried out his name, her inner muscles contracting around him in wonderful spasms as she took him with her over the edge of the world into ecstasy.

He felt complete, more complete than he ever had in his life. But not peaceful. This interlude with Ariana had been magical. But he'd known from the beginning that it could never last for longer than a few hours.

The beginning must be the start of the end.

They both lay panting on the chaise. When she reached to brush back a lock of his hair, he kissed her cheek, then rolled to his side and cradled her against himself.

"I knew that would be wonderful with you," she whispered.

"And with you." He raised his head and saw moisture shimmering in her eyes. "Did I hurt you?" he asked urgently.

"Just a little, right at the beginning."

"I'm sorry."

"Don't be. I wanted to do that for the first time with you. And I'm so glad I did."

How was he going to give her up? He didn't know. But he understood that he couldn't keep her with him for much longer.

She reached to touch his face. "That was so much more than I ever could have imagined."

"Yes." Making love had never meant so much to him. He wanted to share everything he was feeling. But he knew that telling her he'd fallen in love with her in this one long night would only make their parting more painful. So he brought her hand to his lips and kissed her fingers.

"I don't want it to be over," she whispered.

"Neither do I," he answered, admitting that much as he shifted her hand so that he could press a kiss into her palm.

He felt sudden tension shoot through her.

"What?" He sat up, his gaze riveting to the door, as he prepared to face an enemy charging toward them. But no one had discovered their hiding place. They were still alone.

"We could run away," she said in a shaky voice.

"You're kidding, right?"

She made a small sound. "Only partly."

He understood completely. He had always enjoyed women, but he'd never met one he could have imagined spending the rest of his life with. Now he was holding her in his arms, and she was forbidden to him. This interlude never should have happened. Really, his only choice was to deliver Ariana safely back to the people who must be frantically looking for her.

"I want to stay here a little while longer," she murmured.

He moved his arm so that he could look at his watch. It was close to three in the morning, and he knew he shouldn't give in to temptation, but he was helpless to deny her. To deny himself.

"Yes, we've got a little while," he agreed, feeling the precious seconds with her slipping by, each one like a hammer strike against his heart.

AN AIDE CAME STRIDING BACK to Agent Harold Wolf's makeshift command post, his expression resigned.

"Now what?" Harold snapped.

"We have a communication from the State Department. King Frederick of Beau Pays is on his way over here to personally supervise the search for his daughter."

This time Wolf's curse could be heard halfway across Copley Square. "We can't have foreign operatives running around Boston when the situation is already explosive. Tell him to stay home, and we'll inform him as soon as we find his daughter."

"It's too late. He's already taken off."

"How long do we have?"

"Seven hours."

Wolf cursed again. He was short staffed. He needed every man here, combing the building, looking for the vice president. But he wasn't going to be responsible for an international incident.

"Okay. Give the police a direct order to go to that street address where she was last seen," he muttered, knowing that they might or might not respond.

SHANE LAY ON HIS BACK, his fingers knitted with Ariana's.

"Tell me about your life," she said.

His whole life. How long did he have? Ten minutes? He thought for a moment, wondering which details to pick, and knowing he couldn't tell her everything, even if he wanted to. His missions for Eclipse were a secret. Nobody knew the identity of the men of Eclipse. Even Dana Whitley, who worked in the Pentagon by day and relayed assignments to the team by night, didn't know their names. If he were getting married, would he tell his future wife?

He stopped that thought in its tracks. It was completely out of place here tonight. He wasn't going to marry Ariana. He was going to take her back where she belonged. Then he was going on with his life, even if he was having trouble imagining the future without her.

"I live in an underground house," he said.

"You're kidding. A cave?"

"No. I had it built into a hillside, so you can't see it until you're almost on top of it."

"Don't you feel like a bear in a burrow when you're in there?"

"No. It's a lot nicer than an animal den."

"I didn't mean to insult you," she said quickly.

"That's okay. It does have light. From sun tunnels. They're like skylights with special tubing that let in natural light and magnify it. Aboveground they look like ventilator shafts."

"Is your furniture modern?"

"My electronics lab is state of the art. In the living area, the sofas and chairs are contemporary because those are the most comfortable. But they're mixed in with a lot of antique cabinet pieces."

She gave him a considering look. "I wouldn't have thought you'd like antiques."

"This guy is too gauche?"

She blushed. "I might have thought that at first. Now I picture you in a no-nonsense, modern setting."

"I like feeling connected to the past. I like sitting at a desk and imagining a French merchant sitting at the same desk three hundred years ago and writing out his receipts. Only he used a quill pen, and I have a computer."

"Then you'd fit right into my world. We're tied to the past by our traditions, but we take advantage of modern technology and we're always looking toward the future."

They stared at each other. They were skirting dangerous territory. His fitting into her world was impossible, and they both knew it. Before he could point that out, she asked another question.

"What do you do for fun?"

"I like classic movies. And classic cars. I have six in my garage. I've got a 1956 Thunderbird. A 1930's Rolls-Royce. A 1949 Ford. I play chess with people around the world. We each have a board set up and e-mail our opponent our moves."

"My father does that! Maybe you can play him sometime."

"Maybe," he answered, doubting it, so he went on. "I have a fully equipped gym. And I spend a lot of time working out."

She ran her fingers lightly along his arm, stopping to squeeze his biceps. "I can tell."

"And I like tinkering in my lab. Inventing equipment I can use in my work or modifying gear that's already on the market."

Her voice turned husky. "Tell me about your bedroom. I want to picture you there."

Lord, he wanted her there. In his bed. But he kept his voice even as he said, "It's modern, actually. And very spare. I have a slab of walnut for a headboard. A king-sized bed. Low square bedside tables. And drapes on the wall across from the bed, so it looks like there's a floor-to-ceiling window. But the drapes hide the flat TV screen that hangs on the wall. And I have nice warm Berber carpet on the floor, with Turkish area rugs on top."

"No other furniture?"

"It's in the dressing area."

"And you have a luxury bath."

"Yeah. With a steam shower." He shifted so that he could play with a strand of her blond hair. "Enough about my environment. What about *your* bedroom?"

"It's Danish modern. No nonsense."

"What a letdown. I'd already put you in a fairy-tale setting with lots of gold and lots of carved pieces."

"Too extravagant," she said immediately. "I hate the idea of being a stereotypical princess."

"Never! What do *you* do for fun?"

"I don't have much time for it."

The way she said it made his heart contract.

She went on quickly. "There's so much to do, especially since my mother died two years ago."

"I'm sorry."

"I keep busy. Committees. Charities. I lend my name to a lot of good causes because I know it will help raise money. But I don't just sit back and let other people do all the work. When I left home, I was in the middle of planning a job-training program for women that included day care for their children."

"All that's good. But you need time for yourself. Otherwise, you'll burn out."

"I'm starting to realize that," she said in a small voice. "If you were going to be my social director, where would you take me?"

"White-water rafting," he said.

"That sounds like fun."

"And on a Mediterranean cruise in a small yacht. We'd stop at hidden coves where we could swim with nobody bothering us."

She laughed. "We'd have to wear bathing suits in front of the crew."

"Then let's make it a sailboat we can handle by ourselves. Do you know how to sail?"

"No."

"I'll teach you," he said. But when he heard a siren in the distance, he realized he was letting himself get too much into the fantasy of continuing their relationship. "That could be the police looking for you."

"Yes."

"We have to take you back."

"I don't want to go back." She twined her arms

around his neck and pulled him close, then brought her mouth to his for a hard, desperate kiss.

She put her emotions into the kiss. Emotions that matched his. It was so tempting to let her take him under, but he allowed himself to enjoy the contact for only a few seconds. Then he forced himself to raise his head. "If you keep that up, we'll end up making love again."

"That's what I was hoping."

"We can't," he said, forcing himself to be the sensible one when he badly wanted to give in to temptation.

"I know," she whispered, then rolled away from him. "I was hoping you'd let me have my illusions for a few more minutes."

"They weren't illusions."

"Then what?"

"A precious time together."

"Very precious," she agreed.

The quaver in her voice tore at him. But he knew he would only make it harder for the two of them if he didn't do the right thing now.

Maybe her thoughts were running along similar lines, because she dipped her head and climbed off the chaise. Turning her back, she began collecting the clothing she'd scattered around, and he thought she was probably feeling shy about her nudity.

He allowed her as much privacy as he could while he tugged on his own clothing, then gave up the struggle to keep his gaze off her. As he watched, she crossed to a mirror hanging on the wall and started to pull the remaining pins from her hair. He followed her. Even when he knew he shouldn't touch her, he moved in close, helping her remove pins she couldn't see, then combing his fingers through the silky strands so that her beautiful hair hung around her shoulders and down her back in a golden cascade.

She tipped her head to the side, giving herself a critical inspection. "I look like a mess."

"You look beautiful," he answered, lifting her hair so that he could bend and kiss her neck.

When he looked up, she was staring at him in the mirror, and he saw the moisture glistening in her eyes.

He ached to turn her and hold her close. He ached to say that he was never going to let her go. But the forbidden words stayed locked in his heart.

She was the one who broke the contact. She blinked, then hurried back to the chaise, where she fumbled on the floor and found the tennis shoes they'd taken from the church.

Quickly she shoved her feet into the shoes, then looked up, her face set in stark lines.

"Let's go," she said in a gritty voice.

He longed to take her in his arms and kiss her one last time. But he could see she was deliberately distancing herself from him. And he knew that distance was their only real choice.

He had to return her to the real world. But as he thought about the chaos in the city, he looked around, hoping to find something he could use as a weapon if he needed it.

He saw that the mirror hung over a waist-high counter. Farther along he saw a small kitchen area with an under-counter refrigerator, a sink and several drawers and cabinets. He crossed to the kitchen and started opening drawers till he found a couple of kitchen knives. He took the larger one and shoved it into his belt.

Ariana eyed the weapon. "I hope you're not going to need that."

"I was thinking the same thing." He laughed. "I wish I had a gun I wasn't going to need."

They had been safe in here for a few hours. But he took nothing for granted as they prepared to leave the refuge. He made her wait at the entrance to the summer-house while he studied the silent garden. Then he led her across the open space around the pool. When she arrived at the gate, she started to reach for the knob.

But he pulled her hand back. "Wait. Let me go first."

She looked as if she wanted to protest, but she finally stepped back.

He opened the door and peered out into the darkness. The area was clear, but he was still being cautious. He stepped onto the pavement, then scanned the street, startled that the outside world looked much as it had when they'd left a few hours ago. He felt as if he'd lived a lifetime in the summerhouse with Ariana. It wasn't enough, but it would have to do.

"All clear," he called softly.

She came up behind him, just as a bullet plowed into the stone wall inches from his head.

Chapter Fifteen

Shane ducked back inside the garden, slamming the door in the wall behind him, then clicked the lock closed.

"What happened?" she gasped. "I thought we were safe."

"So did I. But somebody's shooting at us. Again."

In the moonlight, her face had turned pale. He gave her arm a quick squeeze, wishing he could do something more reassuring. Instead, he turned, looking at the garden with new eyes. When they'd first come in here, it had seemed like a refuge. Now it felt more like a death trap.

"Come on," he whispered.

He ushered Ariana into the shadows along the wall, then around an elaborate outdoor barbecue grill built into a tiled work surface.

He didn't have to tell her to crouch behind the barrier. He'd found them cover, but he was still cursing as he drew the knife he'd taken from the small kitchen. Lucky he'd thought of it. And lucky these people had built a fortress of an outdoor cooking center.

He hefted the weapon in his hand, judging the

weight and balance. It would be very satisfactory in a close-quarters knife fight, but not so great when the other guy had a gun.

He and Ariana were sprawled on an uneven surface. Reaching down, he found that the area behind the grill was lined with river rocks.

They'd make good missiles. Too bad he didn't have the makings of a slingshot.

"Who's out there?" Ariana whispered.

"It could be the punks who attacked us. Or it could be Shea."

"Him? But how would he find us?"

"I'd like to know."

When he heard a noise, he looked cautiously around the edge of the grill area. As he'd expected, he saw the door in the wall open and the figure of a man step into the garden.

In the darkness, Shane couldn't get a good look at the guy's face, but the man was dressed in coveralls like the ones the gunman had been wearing in Copley Square. He held his gun out in two hands, like a character in a TV cop series.

"Looks like Shea," Shane whispered as he picked up two of the rocks in his free hand.

Their hiding place was only thirty feet from the door in the wall, and he wished to hell there was more distance between Ariana and the gunman.

Was there any way to get around him and out to the street? Not unless they lured him farther into the garden. And even then, there wasn't much maneuvering room since the swimming pool took up a good part of the open area.

He brought his ear close to Ariana's. "I'm going to

throw the rocks to our left. When I do, run to the right and make for the house. Put the corner of the building between you and the shooter. Then get inside."

"How?"

"You'll probably have to break a window, and he'll hear it. But get in, then get out the front door. When you're outside, go down the street. Get away from here."

She picked up two of the rocks. "Where will you be?"

"Right behind you." *I hope,* he silently added. "Ready?"

"Yes."

"Now." He hurled one stone and then the other, sending them flying against the wall. As he'd hoped, a barrage of bullets began pounding the wall. Maybe the guy would use up his ammunition and have to reload. Could Shane jump him then?

Ariana took off, running toward the bulky cover of the house, and he prayed that the ruse would last long enough for them to get into the house.

When the shooting continued, Shane hustled after Ariana, expecting to hear the sound of breaking glass. But all he detected was a series of thumps.

He reached the shadow of the structure just as the man with the gun figured out that the rocks weren't his quarry. The assailant whirled in the other direction and directed his fire toward the building.

Shane felt a bullet whiz past his shoulder. Then another one so close it nearly parted the hair on the top of his head.

Much too close for comfort.

He sped up and careened around the corner just in time to see Ariana smash the rock against the sliding glass door. The stone just bounced back.

She turned to him, her face filled with terror. "I hit it as hard as I can, but it won't break."

Looking along the back wall of the house, he cursed under his breath. The house had obviously been modified in the past few years, and there were no windows at ground level along the back, just sliding glass doors.

"Safety glass. It's hard to break." Grabbing the rock from her, he smashed it against the door surface with all his strength. His success rate was no better than hers. As he braced for the gunman to come roaring around the corner, he searched for something heavier to use as a battering ram.

An expensive cement planter full of geraniums sat beside the door, and he picked it up, grunting as he heaved it against the glass. This time the door cracked. Then, with the characteristic of safety glass, small pieces began falling out of the pane and tinkling to the ground.

Desperate to get Ariana inside, he rammed his shoulder against the vertical surface, bits of glass sticking in his shirt as he enlarged the opening. Around him, he could hear the chips of glass falling and bouncing like large pieces of hail.

"Come on, come on," he muttered. As he pulled on the glass, making a hole large enough to climb through, he kept expecting the guy with the gun to come charging around the corner. Apparently he thought he had them trapped, and he was being cautious.

It seemed as if centuries were passing, but Shane knew they'd only been standing there for a few seconds.

Seeing what he was doing, Ariana helped him, pulling away a large section of the door.

They both worked frantically, and he could see her

lips moving, hear her whispering a prayer. He hoped that God was listening and that he looked favorably on the royal family of Beau Pays.

"Go," he shouted to Ariana when the space was big enough for her to get her shoulders through. "Find the front door. Get out to the street."

She stumbled into what looked like a large family room, then stopped for a minute to get her bearings, before bolting across the rug and disappearing through a doorway at the other side of the room.

Shane followed, through a kitchen, then into a hallway that opened into a vestibule. The large front door had a double lock.

The bottom knob turned easily after he twisted the locking button, but the upper lock was a dead bolt. The kind you worked with a key. And the key was missing.

Cursing their luck, he looked for Ariana. But she had already disappeared down a hallway.

"Go out a window," he called after her. "Hurry."

The dining room was on the far side of the vestibule. He sprinted across the marble floor, looking for a good place to hide. Floor-to-ceiling damask draperies hung on either side of a bay window. He was about to step behind them when he pictured the guy with the gun spraying the room with bullets.

Better to find more substantial cover.

At the far end of the house, he could hear footsteps crunching over glass. When the footsteps stopped, he figured the guy must be thinking about where they'd gone.

Shane hurried through the kitchen, then through a wide archway into a formal living room. The sofas and chairs were grouped around an Oriental rug, and he crossed to one of the sofas and crouched behind it.

An eerie silence reigned over the house—until the sound of an automatic weapon made his throat clog.

Had the bastard found Ariana? Or was he just shooting at random targets hoping to flush them out like game birds in a field?

He wanted to shout to Ariana and ask if she was okay, but giving that much away would be a fatal move. Instead, he crouched behind the sofa, holding his knife at the ready and silently calling out to the guy, hoping he'd come into the living room.

He heard footsteps in the hall, then a blast of gunfire hit the sofa behind which he was hiding.

Shane stayed where he was, thankful that the thick padding had stopped the bullets.

The man crept across the rug, not bothering to hide his intentions. Obviously he thought that if anybody else had a gun, they would have fired by now.

Shane tensed, ready to spring when Shea got within range.

Long seconds ticked by.

Come on. Come on, you bastard.

As he waited for the man to round the sofa, Shane kept one ear cocked for Ariana. Was she out of the house? Was she all right?

Worrying about her was a distraction he didn't need with the assailant bearing down on him, and he forced his concentration back to the man who was now crossing the rug.

He wanted to see what was going on, but he knew any attempt to peek around the sofa would give his location away. So he stayed absolutely still, trying to listen hard, waiting for his optimum chance at the guy.

He saw a figure looming above him, saw an outstretched arm holding a gun. The guy was being too damn cautious. Which meant he was nervous.

When the gun arm swung to the left, Shane leaped up and launched himself from behind the sofa, slashing down with the knife as he sprang forward. But he was two beats too far away, and the frantic movement gave the assailant a few seconds notice. The man sprang back, avoiding the knife blade by inches as he started shooting again.

Shane rolled to his left, making for one of the chairs, as bullets crashed into the wall, the woodwork and the window behind him.

"You're a dead man," Shea growled. "And the princess is next."

The man raised his gun, obviously savoring the moment of victory. Shane prepared to make a desperate leap at him with the knife. Maybe he could slit the bastard's throat before he went down for good himself.

Before the man could fire again, two blasts from another gun split the air.

The assailant whirled, his finger pressing the trigger, spraying bullets toward the wide archway. But he was the one who screamed and fell to the floor.

Looking up, Shane saw Ariana step from around the edge of the doorway and advance with a pistol in her hand. She looked as dazed as he felt—and at the same time triumphant.

He stared at her, hardly able to believe the evidence of his own eyes. Somehow she'd found a weapon and brought the bastard down.

"Where did you get that gun?" he gasped.

She dragged in a breath and let it out, steadying herself before answering. "In a drawer in the office. My father keeps a pistol in his desk drawer. I looked there and found one."

"Lucky for us."

"We were due some luck," she answered, keeping the weapon trained on the man who had fallen.

Shea was still dangerous. And when he moved, Shane stepped on his gun hand, and he screamed.

"Keep him covered," Shane directed.

"A pleasure."

After taking the weapon away from the assailant, Shane bent to inspect the man's injury. Bright arterial blood spurted across the sleeve of his shirt. If they didn't do something quickly, the bastard was going to die. Which wouldn't be such a bad idea, except that Shane wanted information.

Standing, he looked around.

"What?" Ariana breathed.

"We need something for a tourniquet or he'll bleed out."

Ariana looked around the room, then pointed to the draperies. "One of the tiebacks?"

"Yeah." He sprinted to the sliding glass door and ripped down one of the silken cords, then wrapped it tightly around the man's upper arm, tying the ends together. It made a perfect tourniquet.

The man rolled his head weakly toward Shane, and he saw a face he recognized. Though not the exact same face from his past, the guy looked a lot like Liam Shea had looked eleven years ago, and Shane knew his assumption was correct. This had to be one of Liam's sons.

"Why?" Shane growled.

"I don't have to tell you a damn thing," the man bit out, his voice laced with pain.

Shane gave him a parody of a smile. "The important thing is that you know you've lost."

"That's what you think," the assailant answered. "There's a lot more to come."

Was that bravado speaking—or reality?

"Like what?"

"A very explosive finish to the evening," he said, then lay back and closed his eyes.

Shane crouched over Liam's son, wanting to shake the truth out of him. Instead he tried another tactic. Softening his voice, he said, "It will go better for you if you talk."

"Don't give me that crap."

"I know who you are. You have to be one of Liam Shea's sons. Which one are you? Colin, Finn or Aidan?"

The man's lips twitched, but he remained silent.

"Why did you agree to such a murderous plan?"

The man finally spoke. But his answer wasn't very helpful. "Family loyalty."

"Family loyalty is going to get you convicted of murder."

"Maybe not."

The smug satisfaction in the injured man's voice made Shane want to throttle him.

Ariana broke into the conversation. "We have to call an ambulance."

Shane looked down at the man who had tried so hard to kill them, wondering why she cared about saving this guy.

She answered his unspoken question. "I want a trial. I want the world to know what he did in the Hancock Tower, in the church and here."

"Too bad there's no death penalty in Massachusetts," Shane growled.

At the same time, he was thinking about what a trial would mean. It would bring Ariana back here.

He reached for his cell phone to call an ambulance and realized he didn't have it, or any of the other personal items he'd brought from the reception.

"We may be able to use a cell phone if we can find one."

"I'll go look," Ariana volunteered. "You watch him."

"Okay."

She had just disappeared down the hall when the front door burst open with a resounding crack.

SHANE WATCHED UNIFORMED COPS pour into the room. They were followed by a man in his forties with close-cropped brown hair. He was wearing a rumpled business suit, and Shane figured he must be the detective in charge.

Shane gave the cops a professional appraisal. They had guns drawn, and none of them looked exactly friendly. He could see that they were still trying to figure out the situation, and they weren't taking any chances on getting it wrong.

One of the uniforms knelt beside the man on the floor and eyed the blood on his shirt and the tourniquet. "He's in bad shape. What happened to him?"

Before Shane could answer, the injured man stirred, his gaze flicking to Shane, then to the cop who bent over him. "Me and my partner came in to rob the place, and we got into an argument."

"Now wait a damn minute," Shane objected.

"He shot me. And he was going to leave me here," Shea gasped out.

This time, Shane addressed himself directly to the

detective. "He's lying. He was trying to kill us, with the gun on the floor. I kicked it out of his reach. You'll find his fingerprints on the gun, not mine. You'll find powder residue on his hand, not mine. And you'll find bullets and shell casings from his gun sprayed all over the place in here and in the garden."

"He was trying to kill us, and I shot him." The clarification came from Ariana who had come down the hall and was standing in the doorway, still holding the gun.

Two uniformed officers whirled toward her and immediately focused on the weapon in her hand.

"Stop where you are. Drop the gun and lie on the floor," one of them shouted.

Shane's heart leaped into his throat as he sized up the situation. These cops didn't know she was the heir to the throne of Beau Pays. All they knew was that she held a gun in her hand.

"Ariana, do what he says," he called to her.

"I…"

He knew this woman. She was brave and loyal and highly intelligent, with a streak of royal stubbornness she'd inherited from her father.

He prayed that she wasn't going to let that prevent her from obeying.

Chapter Sixteen

Ariana felt the blood drain from her face. Through her panic she heard Shane's pleading voice. "They don't know who you are. All they know is that you have a gun. So do what he says!"

She did, dropping the gun, then lying down.

Two of the officers rushed forward. After one kicked the gun away, the other pulled her hands behind her back and cuffed them, then started to search her.

"You," the detective said to Shane. "Get down on the floor. Spread 'em."

Shane got down, still looking at her as one of the officers began to search him.

She tried to tell the police who she was, but the detective told her to shut up.

The uniform finished her search, then stood. "She's clean."

Two of the officers helped her to her feet, where she gave the detective a murderous look. She tried to free her hands, but the cuffs held her fast.

She couldn't believe this was happening to her. To Shane.

The detective reached into his pocket and pulled out

a photograph, then a flashlight. He shone the light on the picture, then on Ariana, comparing the two.

"What's your name?" he demanded.

She squared her shoulders and straightened her spine. "I am Princess Ariana of Beau Pays."

"What is your birthday?"

"April twenty-fifth," she said.

"And your mother's maiden name?"

"Eleanore of Layden."

"You know your facts. But we'll have to sort this out at the station house."

Ariana wanted to scream at these police officers that they were making a terrible mistake. She knew she and Shane were still in danger, so she kept her lips pressed together and tried to call on the discipline that had been drummed into her.

Still, a sick feeling rose in her throat as she watched one of the policemen pat down Shane's front pocket. He made a clucking sound, then pulled out the Beau Pays sapphire.

"Well, well," he said, holding it up. "It looks like you got some loot while you were here. What's this?"

Ariana couldn't stop herself from speaking. "It didn't come from this house. That's a valuable jewel from my country that was on display at the reception at the Hancock Tower."

"And we stole it," the Shea brother wheezed.

"No!" Ariana's outrage bubbled over. Desperately she cast around for the best possible wording and said, "Shane rescued it."

Shea made a snorting sound. "And pigs can fly."

She hated him as she had never hated anyone in her life, but she gave him points for mendacity and persistence. As long as he kept throwing in lying comments, he was going to keep the police off balance and make the situation seem totally different from reality.

Shane remained motionless on the floor as one of the officers cuffed his hands behind his back and helped him up.

The other stuffed the sapphire into a plastic bag.

Ariana had to clench her hands into fists to keep herself from screaming.

Her eyes met Shane's for an instant before he looked quickly away, and she felt her stomach clench. They were standing here, cuffed like common criminals. And there was nothing they could do about it.

She ached to use her royal position to make these men bend to her will. She had seen and heard her father use his kingly authority on numerous occasions. She herself had used the same techniques when she'd been in inconvenient situations in her own country.

But she wasn't back in Beau Pays with hundreds of years of royal tradition backing her up. This was the United States. And she wasn't dealing with an inconvenience. This was a life-or-death situation. If she did or said the wrong thing, she or Shane could get hurt.

A stir at the front of house made her look up. Paramedics wheeling a stretcher rushed into the room and bent over the man on the floor.

She watched them working over him, thinking that if she'd killed him, he wouldn't be telling his lies, and they wouldn't be in this fix.

The horrible thought brought her up short. She had been fighting for Shane's life. But now that the emergency was over, she thanked God that she hadn't killed the man. No matter what he had done, she didn't want his death on her conscience.

One of the medics hung a bag of clear liquid on a pole while the other inserted a needle into the injured man's vein.

"How is he?" the detective asked.

"He's lost a lot of blood. And his pressure's low."

"I want him kept under guard in the emergency room and anywhere else he goes in the hospital," the man in charge ordered. "I don't want anyone besides the medical staff near him unless they have written authorization."

"Yes, sir."

"And make sure you don't get someone posing as a doctor or nurse," Shane muttered, loud enough for everyone to hear.

The detective blanched—then repeated the advice to the medics.

"Yes, sir," they said again.

After the paramedics wheeled Shea out, the detective stepped toward Ariana. "I'm going to uncuff you because you match the description of the princess who is missing. And you know your facts."

One of the officers unlocked the cuffs, and she pulled her hands to her front, then rubbed her wrists.

"Because I *am* the princess who is missing." She gave the man in the rumpled suit a direct look. "What is your name?" she inquired.

"Detective Tyndall."

"Well, Detective Tyndall, I think you'd better let the State Department know that I'm safe. Before you end up in the middle of an international incident."

"Don't threaten me," he said. "What are you doing in this house?"

"The wounded man you took away is one of the three

sons of Liam Shea. They and their father took the president of the United States and a roomful of dignitaries hostage on the top floor of the Hancock Tower. I was one of those hostages, and Shane Peters…" She paused and gestured toward him. "Shane Peters got me to safety."

Ignoring the comment, the detective asked another question. "Do you have any idea what generated the hostage situation?"

"Liam Shea, the father, was convicted of insubordination during a raid in Barik eleven years ago. He wanted to get revenge on the other men who were on the raid with him."

"An odd way of doing it."

"It mirrors the situation eleven years ago."

Detective Tyndall glanced at Shane. "Did he tell you that?"

She felt suddenly trapped. "Yes."

"Yeah, well, we don't know if any of that is true." He gave her a speculative look. "According to the information I was given, you were supposed to leave in a helicopter. What are you doing wandering around Boston in a blackout?"

She felt her chest tighten, but she kept her gaze even. "Shea shot at us in Copley Square. We had to run into the church. He followed us inside and we escaped through a back door."

"King Frederick is worried about his daughter."

"My father," she gasped.

The detective kept talking. "We've got a citywide blackout, citizens going berserk. We should have every man on the force out there. But we had to divert valuable resources to finding you."

She felt her face heat as he asked, "Where were you all this time?"

Her face grew even hotter when she thought about what she and Shane had been doing, but she managed to keep her composure.

"We were hiding out," she said in a low voice, then raised her chin. "Shane Peters got me away from Copley Square. He saved my life. I want him released."

Tyndall looked toward Shane, then back to her. "You're sure this is Peters?"

"Yes."

He beckoned toward the officer who had searched Shane. "Did you find any identification on this man?"

"No, sir."

Ariana struggled to keep her tone even. "He lost his wallet and his cell phone, in the church. We had to change our clothes…"

"Oh yeah?"

She could imagine what the detective was thinking. Unfortunately, she could also imagine newspaper headlines. Beau Pays Princess Accused of Robbing Church, Breaking and Entering in Boston Blackout."

Using her best princess voice, she said, "We were dressed for a fancy reception when we escaped from the gunman. We couldn't run around the city looking like that. So we put on clothing from the church collection. We'll be glad to replace the items and make a sizable donation to the church."

She glanced at Shane for confirmation.

"Yeah, we'll make a donation," he said, but he sounded as if he wasn't betting that they'd get the chance.

Just then one of the uniformed officers came back

into the room. "The garden's full of shell casings. And the barbecue is shot up."

"And the corner of the house," Shane added.

"And a sliding glass door in back is bashed in," the officer continued.

"We broke in to get away from the gunman," Ariana said quickly.

The detective sighed. "We'd better sort this out at the station house."

One of the men grabbed Shane's arm, and she saw his body go rigid and his expression darken. For a terrible moment she thought he was going to wrench himself away and start running. Then, to her vast relief, he got control of himself. He gave her a long penetrating look, then mouthed the words "Call Ty," before allowing the policeman to lead him to the door.

Call Ty, she repeated. *Ty.* And then she remembered. His friend, the Secret Service agent.

"Can I make a phone call?" she asked.

"To whom?"

"To Secret Service Agent Ty Jones. He was with the vice president at the Hancock Tower. I saw him speaking to Shane Peters at the reception, so I know he can identify him."

When Tyndall hesitated, Ariana finally reached the end of her patience. "I'd appreciate your letting me locate him," she said in a tone that elevated her several steps above the men around her.

"How are you going to get him?"

"Put me through to the Secret Service." She held her breath, waiting to see if Tyndall would give her that much consideration. After what felt like centuries, he pulled a cell phone from his pocket. But instead of handing it to her, he began punching in numbers. Then, giving her a narrow-eyed look, he moved away where she couldn't hear what he was saying.

Her breath grew shallow as she watched his tense body language.

When he came back, his expression was grim. "Agent Jones has his hands full at the moment. He may or may not be able to come down to the station house."

Screams of frustration clogged her throat, held back by years of self-control training. Instead, she gave Tyndall a direct look and said, "Agent Jones is a friend of Mr. Peters. He'll come as soon as he can."

"Believe me, I'd like to clear this up," Tyndall said, his voice almost kind.

Was he finally feeling sorry for her? Had someone on the phone told him what they'd been through up on the sixtieth floor of the Hancock Tower?

She might have asked, but she was starting to think that the less she gave away, the better.

So she silently followed Tyndall outside and toward one of the patrol cars.

When she didn't see Shane inside, panic clawed at her. Then she spotted him in the car behind hers.

She had spent countless hours of her life driving in motorcades through her country and in foreign locations during state visits.

Tonight's trip through the darkened streets felt like the longest journey of her life. They drove in a tight convoy of four police cars. As she looked out the window, she saw a scene out of a nightmare.

Some vehicles had crashed into each other and into lampposts. Down the block, people were running through the streets, piles of groceries and other goods in their arms. And in the distance, a fire lit up the sky.

The city was out of control and on the edge of panic, and these men were doing the best they could to keep the situation from deteriorating further.

"I guess you're having a difficult time tonight," she said in a quiet voice.

Detective Tyndall grunted. "Yeah. Seems like half the city is out looting and shooting. The other half is hunkered down, thinking this is a terrorist attack."

"Did they give you any information about the hostage situation at the Hancock Tower?"

"Some," he answered laconically, and she knew that he wasn't going to give her anything she could use.

They reached a solidly built stone structure where emergency lights illuminated the barred windows and grimy walls. The lights also gave her a clear view of Shane and the two officers who helped him from the back of the police cruiser. She knew they were going to arrest him, and she knew that stain would always be on his record, even if it was ultimately proven that he had done nothing wrong.

This misadventure could be a personal disaster for him and a professional disaster for his security business. And all because he'd been trying to protect her.

She wanted to shout out that this was her fault. But she knew it would ultimately make things worse. So she stood there watching two officers march Shane up a short flight of stone steps.

One of them reached for the knob, then froze as a screeching sound split the air. She turned to see a black car shoot out of the darkness and pull up in front of the police station.

A man jumped out and charged up the steps.

"Agent Jones. Secret Service," he shouted, holding out a leather case with his badge.

Everybody stopped in their tracks.

"I have identification for this man, Shane Peters," he added as he pulled a sheet of paper out of his pocket. "This is a photocopy of Peters's driver's license. I also have a letter from the president of the United States personally commending Mr. Peters for his heroism tonight. The president wants him released from custody immediately."

"Talk about going to the top," Tyndall muttered.

Ty turned to him. "Are you in charge?" he asked.

"Yes."

Ty hurried toward him and handed over the papers.

Tyndall looked at them, then turned to the officers who held Shane.

"Take the cuffs off him," he said.

"Thank you," Ariana whispered. She wanted to run to Shane and throw her arms around his neck, but she understood that she couldn't behave that way in public.

Instead she turned to Ty Jones. "Thank you," she said again.

"I'm glad I could get here in time." He pulled more papers from his briefcase. "And this is identification for Princess Ariana of Beau Pays."

She blinked. She'd forgotten that her own identity could also be in question. But Ty Jones had remembered, and he had cleared that up, too.

After turning over the papers, he walked to Shane, and the two of them shook hands stiffly, then began talking in low voices. That was more than Ariana could take. She'd been through hell with these two men, and she wanted to know what Ty had found out. Leaving Tyndall's side, she walked up the steps.

"Tell me what happened," she said.

Ty turned to her. "Are you all right?"

"Yes. Thanks to Shane."

"We need to get you out of the city."

"After they make a statement," Tyndall broke in. "We have to make a report on the break-in and the shooting."

Ariana wanted to object. They'd been through so much, and she didn't want to waste any more time with the police.

But Shane gave her a firm look. "We'd better make an official report so the correct version gets on the record."

She considered the advice and realized he was right. So she nodded, and they both followed Tyndall inside.

"I'll expedite this," he said after he'd led them down a short hallway. "We have the guy's weapon. We can match it to the bullets all over the house and at the church."

"Thank you," she murmured.

"I'd like you to each write up a separate report," he said.

Her stomach clenched. She'd thought she and Shane could confer. But apparently the detective wanted to make sure their stories matched.

Shane caught her expression. "Just write what happened. You'll be fine," he said.

"Okay."

They were in the police station for over an hour. Finally, Tyndall told them they were free to go.

Although Ariana could barely stand to be in the station house another minute, she forced herself to take a few more minutes. Turning to Tyndall, she said, "Thank you so much. We'd be in a lot of trouble if you hadn't come along. My father will want to thank you for your service to me. I'm sure he'll want to call you."

"Maybe he can speak to me in person," the detective answered.

"What?"

"He's on his way to Boston."

"No!"

"You don't want to see him?"

Recovering her equanimity, she said, "I came to Boston because he was ill. He shouldn't be traveling." She stopped and swallowed. "When is he expected to arrive?"

The detective looked at his watch. "Four and a half hours."

She breathed out a small sigh. The timetable gave her some wiggle room. But maybe she didn't have as much time as she needed.

Her heart had started to pound, and she felt as nervous as when they'd been hiding in the church. Her father had never been a patient man, and she knew he worried about her too much since the death of her brother and then her mother. She hated to think what he would do when she had to speak to him.

As if he were reading her mind, Tyndall said, "I may be able to patch you in to his plane."

"Does he know I'm all right?" she asked.

"Yes."

"In that case, I don't have to speak to him immediately," she said, then asked in a quiet but firm voice, "Where am I supposed to meet him?"

"At Otis Air Force Base."

"Merci." She gave the man a quick smile which she thought probably looked forced. "If you don't mind, I'd like to be able to give the Beau Pays sapphire back to him."

The detective looked flustered, since that detail had apparently slipped his mind. "The sapphire. Yeah. I forgot about that. Give me a minute."

He rushed off and spoke to the uniformed officer who had put the jewel into an evidence bag.

Moments later he was back and handing her the national treasure.

"Thank you so much," she said, then turned to Shane. "Can you keep this safe for me?"

"Certainly," he answered without missing a beat. As he put the jewel back into his pocket, he asked, "Is everything okay?"

"Yes," she managed to say, even when she knew that the next few hours were going to be as difficult as the last few.

When they reached Ty's vehicle, he got into the driver's seat.

After a moment's hesitation, Shane climbed into the backseat with her. She needed to feel connected with him, wanted to reach for his hand, but she couldn't do that in front of Ty. Instead, she clasped her hands in her lap before asking the Secret Service agent, "Do you know which one of the brothers went after us?"

"We believe it's Colin."

"And what about Vice President Davis?"

Ty's face darkened. "He's still missing."

"You searched the building?"

"Yes. He wasn't there."

"Did you find out if that blood in the stairwell was from him?"

"We had to fly it to a lab outside the city. We're waiting for the results."

She studied his worried face. "I'm sorry you can't get any information."

"I was supposed to keep him safe," Ty bit out.

"You didn't have control over what happened tonight," she said softly. "Liam Shea and his sons went to a lot of trouble to set up tonight's scenario. They had everything planned down to the last detail."

"And you two screwed up his plans, big time. I'm relieved you're safe. I was worried when I found out you didn't get on the chopper."

"Sorry. That was my fault," she and Shane said at the same time.

"We can assign blame later," the agent said. "Meanwhile, I have a piece of good news for you," he said, turning to Ariana.

He had said *good news,* but she couldn't stop her stomach from tightening.

"Your bodyguard, Manfred Werner, is going to make it."

She stared at him in shock. "I—I thought he was dead."

"So did the Sheas. They left him on the floor, and he had sense enough to play dead. He was wearing a Kevlar vest, and that saved his life."

"Thank God," she breathed.

Shane covered her hand with his. Not caring if Ty was watching, she turned her hand up and knitted her fingers with Shane's. When he tightened his grip on her, she returned the pressure.

"I was horrified when I thought he'd been killed," she murmured. "Thank you so much for telling me."

"Well, he has a leg wound, and his chest is badly bruised from the rounds he took."

"Yes."

They were all silent for several moments. Then Shane asked, "What about the power plant? Is the utility company making any progress on repairing it?"

"They're working on it. But it's going to be off-line for a couple of days."

Shane looked out the window, toward the darkened city, then toward the police station. "I feel sorry for the Boston cops."

"The crime wave will subside when the sun comes up," Ty said.

"And start up again tomorrow night," Shane said.

Before Ty could answer, a long black limousine pulled into the street in front of the police station, and a uniformed driver got out. "I'm supposed to pick up Princess Ariana of Beau Pays," he said in a loud voice, addressing nobody in particular.

"Let me make sure he's legit," Ty said, then climbed out of their car and walked toward the man. "Secret Service Agent Ty Jones. I'd like to see your identification."

"Of course," the driver said, reaching into his pocket and bringing out a driver's license along with a folded sheet of paper.

Ty pulled out a flashlight and carefully examined the man's credentials.

Ariana waited with her stomach tied in knots.

Beside her, Shane let go of her hand and shifted in his seat.

She went rigid as she anticipated his next words.

Clearing his throat, he said, "I guess this is where we say goodbye."

Chapter Seventeen

"No!" Ariana gasped.

In response to her outburst, Shane gave her a piercing look.

She swallowed hard and struggled for calm. She'd been dreading this moment since they'd left the summerhouse. They'd been pretty busy since then, and she hadn't been able to settle on a strategy. Now she hoped that appealing to Shane's protective instincts might be the best way to go.

Making her voice just a little trembly, she said, "I'd feel safer if you stayed with me until I have to leave the city."

As he considered her request, she held her breath.

"Let's hope your safety's no longer an issue," he said stiffly, and she knew he was seeing her as Princess Ariana again.

Her heart was blocking her windpipe, but she managed to say, "Please…don't leave yet."

He shifted in his seat. "Won't that just make things worse?"

"I hope not."

"All right, then."

She let out the breath she'd been holding. *"Merci."*

They both climbed out of Ty's car and into the waiting limousine. Once the driver had started the engine, she pressed the control that closed the opaque window between the passenger compartment and the front seat.

Shane was sitting rigidly beside her. "What's that for?"

"I need to talk to you."

When she reached out and touched his shoulder, he jumped.

"Not a good idea to get too close," he said, his voice gritty.

"I think you're wrong," she answered.

"About what? There's no future for us," he said, making the words very clear and distinct.

"I see you can't speak frankly."

"I'm trying my damnedest to do just that. If you can't face reality, somebody has to."

She had never allowed herself a personal relationship with a man who wasn't part of her family. Not until she had met Shane Peters. She'd gotten to know him, to admire him. When they'd made love, it had been the most emotionally fulfilling experience of her life.

As they sat in the backseat of the limousine, she realized that they had slipped into stereotyped roles— the unreachable princess and the commoner. And she was the only one who could bridge the gap that had sprung up between them.

"We need to bring this back to a personal level," she said softly.

"Don't!"

"If I make a fool of myself, at least I'll never have to see you again. But I want you to know that I'm having trouble imagining a future without you. I think you

Americans have an expression—the bottom line." She swallowed. "The bottom line for me is that I want you to come back to Beau Pays with me."

She saw intense emotions chase themselves across his features, but his words were sharp. "You're engaged to another man," he said, punching out the words.

"I was engaged, yes. But I can't marry Jean Claude. I'd be living a lie. If I made love with him, I'd be thinking about you."

"I don't want to hear you say that."

"But it's the truth. I've gotten closer to you tonight than I ever got to him. I kept him at arm's length, and he allowed that. I realize now that he was flattered by the idea of marrying me, even though he didn't have any strong feelings for me. But you do."

She slid across the space between them and wrapped her arms around him.

"Ariana," he gasped, just before she covered his lips with hers. He was a man with a strong will, and she felt his resistance. But she didn't break the kiss. As she moved her lips against his, she felt resistance crumple. Soon he was returning the kiss, urgently, possessively.

In a secret part of her mind, she had feared that he didn't want her. That he had only been responding to a crazy situation that gave him possession of a princess for one night.

To her vast relief, she had found out that wasn't the problem. He had tried his best to be strong, to do the right thing—for both of them.

She raised her head and pulled far enough away so that she could look up at him. In a voice she couldn't quite hold steady, she said, "Shane, I love you. I can't imagine my life without you."

"You just met me."

Somehow she managed to make herself say, "Am I wrong about the way you feel? If I am, then I guess I've made a fool of myself after all."

He cursed under his breath, then gathered her close. "You know I love you," he growled. "I fell in love with you when I saw you standing on the other side of the reception room."

"Thank God," she breathed.

"But we have to be realistic. You're a princess. I came from a dysfunctional family that lived on the wrong side of the tracks."

"That may be where you came from. But you made yourself into a security expert and a millionaire."

"That doesn't make me a suitable husband for the heir to the throne of Beau Pays."

"I think it does."

She saw from his expression that he wasn't going to cave in yet.

"Maybe you don't have a choice about whom you marry," he said.

"I'm going to make sure I do."

She could still feel his hesitation. "Do I have to seduce you again?" she asked, taking his hand and kissing his fingertips before lowering them to her breast, sliding them over her erect nipple. "Look what you do to me. Just your touch."

He shuddered "You're not playing fair."

"I'll do whatever it takes to convince you."

He lifted his hand away from her, and she felt her insides clench. But instead of moving away, he slung his arm around her shoulder and pulled her closer.

"I love you," he said, his voice soft and intimate.

"But we both have to be realists. Five years from now we could end up hating each other."

"Why?" she challenged.

"Because I wouldn't be any good at playing the part of a ceremonial husband. I can't sit around a palace while you go to committee meetings. And I can't spend my working life going to hospital openings and flower shows walking two paces behind you."

"I'd never ask you to be a…a lapdog. I know that kind of life would poison our relationship. I'd expect you to keep up your business."

He gave her a direct look. "If I work as a security expert, I'll have to be away on assignments when I'm installing systems."

"I understand that."

"You're not just agreeing because you want me to go along with your plans?"

"I wouldn't do that." She kept her gaze steady. "I know you too well. I feel like we lived half a lifetime together tonight."

"Yes."

"I understand that trying to be a ceremonial husband would kill your spirit."

He heaved in a breath and let it out slowly. "You're tempting me beyond endurance."

"Thank God."

"But I'm not going to agree until we get your father's permission."

She felt her mouth go dry, but she realized he was right. Her father was the king, and he could still make it impossible for her to have the man she loved.

"All right," she said in a small voice.

The door compartment beside her housed a cell

phone, among other amenities. Picking it up, she dialed the code that would give her a connection to the palace.

"Hans?" she said, when her father's private secretary came on the line.

"Your Majesty," the man said as soon as he recognized her voice. "We were so worried about you."

"I'm fine. But I need to speak to my father. Can you get me a connection to him?"

"Certainly."

She sat there with her heart pounding and reached for Shane's hand to steady herself. She had been taught diplomacy. The lessons had been just a theory. Now she was facing a crucial test of her training.

When her father came on the line, she hung on to Shane with a death grip.

"Ariana? Are you all right?"

"I'm fine," she repeated, then added, "thanks to Shane Peters."

"Shane Peters. My old friend?" her father asked.

"Yes. He was at the reception. He's the only reason I'm not dead."

Her father made a strangled sound. "It's horrible to think of you caught in that trap."

"Did they tell you it was Liam Shea and his sons who took us captive?"

"Yes. Did it have something to do with Barik?"

"Yes. I can tell you more about it later. The important point is that Shane got me out. He hid me from Shea and his sons when they told the guests they were going to start killing someone every ten minutes—starting with me."

Her father gasped.

"I'm all right. Because of Shane."

"He's a good man to have around in an emergency," her father said, and she heard tears in his voice.

Ariana knew when to press her advantage. "Shane didn't just rescue me. He rescued the Beau Pays sapphire. We have it with us."

"We?"

"Yes. He's here with me."

"Why didn't you say so? Let me speak to him. I want to thank him for saving my daughter and the sapphire."

She felt the tension radiating from Shane, and she knew he could hear the conversation.

"In a minute," she said, then felt herself swallow hard. "He's here because I asked him to marry me."

She heard her father's exclamation of shock.

"That's—"

Before he could say anything he couldn't take back, she quickly finished the sentence. "A surprise to you. I understand why. You're just hearing the news under very difficult circumstances. But I've thought very hard about the consequences."

"You've only known the man for a few hours!" her father said, using the same argument that Shane had given her.

"Yes. But you've known him for years. You know his character. You know his abilities. You know he has honor and integrity."

She watched Shane's face contort, and she was sure he was thinking about the way he'd stolen the sapphire.

She wondered if she'd gone too far when her father's tone turned patient. A bad sign. At the moment, she'd rather face his anger. "And I know he might have trouble fitting into the rigid life of your consort."

"I think Shane and I can work that out together."

"Ariana, you must marry for life. I'm not going to have the stain of a divorce on our family."

"You won't."

Her father had taught her to stand up for her people. He had also taught her eloquence. Tonight she was standing up for herself—and using every persuasive technique she had ever learned. "After we escaped from the tower, one of the Shea brothers came after us. Shane and I worked together to save our lives. We got to understand each other very well. The danger we shared was a shortcut to a very solid relationship. And that made me realize that I'll be a far better queen if I have a man beside me I know I can count on in every way. He's perfect for me." She laughed. "And you'll get something out of it, too. He showed me the security for the sapphire was sadly lacking. But if he's in Beau Pays with me, we'll have one of the world's top security experts on our staff—for a nominal fee." She glanced at Shane and saw him give her a surprised look.

"Do you agree to that?" she mouthed.

"Of course."

"Let me speak to him," her father said, using the tone that meant he expected to be obeyed. She went rigid, but Shane reached for the phone and pried it out of her stiff fingers.

"Did you hear all that?" the king asked.

"Yes, sir."

"Do you love my daughter?"

"Yes, sir."

"And you think you can live in the fishbowl of a European court?"

"If I can continue my security business and use my work as a way to keep up my old connections."

"You're making conditions."

"I have to. Otherwise the marriage won't work."

"You always knew your own mind."

"Yes, sir."

The long pause at the other end of the line made Ariana's breath freeze in her lungs. She knew that pause. It came before King Frederick said something of utmost importance.

"Shane, I've always admired you. I admire my daughter, too."

She felt as if she were standing on the edge of a high cliff with the wind whistling around her as she waited for her father's next words to Shane.

"And I know Ariana has a level head. If she thinks this is the best course for herself and for Beau Pays, then I believe her."

She had just breathed out a sigh when Shane spoiled her feeling of relief.

"I don't want to push you into anything," he said. "Our marriage would affect your kingdom on the highest level."

Ariana made a strangled sound. "Whose side are you on, anyway?" she asked.

"I have to give him a chance to think about this."

"Are you trying to figure out a way to back out of marrying me?" she demanded.

"No."

Ariana was so focused on Shane that she forgot that her father was listening, until he cleared his throat.

"Is this your first fight?" King Frederick asked.

"No," they both said.

"Then I'll be offering congratulations in person in…" Her father paused and spoke to someone in the background. "In three hours."

"We'll be waiting for you," Ariana said.

Shane handed the phone to Ariana, who said goodbye to her father, then clicked off.

When she had replaced the instrument, she turned to Shane. "Are you satisfied that he's agreed?"

"Yes."

Before they could continue the conversation, the speaker inside the passenger compartment cracked to life.

"Your Highness, we've arrived at the safe house where you can wait for your father's plane to land," the limousine driver said.

Shane was the one who answered. "Thank you. We'll be in here for a little while. Why don't you go in and relax."

"Thank you, sir."

The intercom clicked off. Then the driver's door opened and closed again.

They were parked under an emergency light, so Ariana could see the interior of the car through the blackout windows.

When she turned back to Shane, she studied the sudden tension in his face. "What does that expression mean?"

"There's something I need to tell you."

He sounded so grave that her throat tightened. "Something bad?" she managed to ask.

"Something you need to know. A secret part of my life."

She felt her breath hitch. "You don't go around stealing jewels for a living, do you?"

"No. But I belong to a clandestine organization that takes on special jobs the CIA, FBI and Special Forces won't touch. Nobody but the other men who work with me know who we are. Even our Pentagon contact doesn't have our names."

"You're warning me that you might be going into danger."

"Yes, but I know how to take care of myself."

"And you're giving me the information in case this changes my decision."

He nodded tightly.

"Well, thank you for telling me," she answered, then pulled him close and pressed her face to his shoulder. "You were awfully good at saving our lives. I should have known you were still in the game."

"Does that worry you?"

"Some. But it makes our life together all the more precious."

"You are one remarkable princess."

She snuggled against him and felt him stroke his fingers through her hair before tipping her face up so that their eyes could meet.

He was smiling as he said, "Maybe we should start working out the details of our new life together."

"Here?"

"You said your time isn't your own. That you have a lot of state functions and other duties. You've learned what you need to know to fill your official role, but you obviously need some training in relaxation techniques and arranging quality time for yourself."

She saw his lips quirk as he said that last part.

Tipping her head to the side, she asked, "Are you teasing me?"

"I hope not."

He pulled her to him, then slanted his lips over hers, playing with her mouth in a way that made her breath quicken. She was instantly hot and needy, but she managed to say, "We can't make love here."

"Oh yeah?" he answered, sliding his hand under her shirt and finding the hard peak of her nipple, which he proceeded to stiffen even more with his thumb and fingers.

Her breath was shaky, but she managed to say, "Aren't you forgetting something?"

"Am I?"

She reached out and pushed the button that locked the doors. "You're the one who's supposed to be the security expert."

"I think I just learned a lesson from my new apprentice."

They grinned at each other, then she sobered.

"What?"

"Can we really do this here?"

"We can do anything you want, Your Royal Highness. Highness," he mused as he began to unbutton her shirt. "What exactly does that mean?"

"When I was little, I thought it had something to do with my bottom."

He laughed out loud, then hugged her to him. "I love finding new reasons why I love you."

He brought his mouth back to hers, kissing her with a hunger that fueled her own arousal.

Before she knew it, he had her shirt off and had lowered his face to her breasts, pleasuring one nipple with his lips and tongue before sucking it into his mouth and playing the other with his strong fingers.

When he lifted his head, she pushed up his shirt,

stroking the wonderful expanse of his chest, then mirroring what he had done to her, elated when she felt his reaction.

"You like that."

"I like everything you do to me."

She took that as an invitation. She'd been shy with him the first time they'd made love. Now she murmured, "Lie down."

"You're exercising your royal prerogative?"

"Yes."

He stretched out on the wide leather seat, his long legs hanging off to the side.

Leaning over him, she unsnapped his jeans, then lowered his zipper. Before she could lose her nerve, she reached under his shorts and clasped him in her hand. He was hard and heavy, and she stroked her hand along his length.

"Sweetheart, that feels good. Too good."

She pushed his shorts out of the way, gazing down at his magnificent sex.

"Last time, when you asked me to take off my jeans, you wanted me busy, didn't you? You didn't want me to look at you and see how big you are."

"Yeah."

"A good move. I would have been afraid you wouldn't fit inside me."

"But we've already found out that we fit together perfectly." As he spoke, he unsnapped her jeans, lowered the zipper and pushed the garment down. His fingers caressed the territory he had bared, dipping into her folds, sending heat shooting through her.

He knew how to touch her, how to arouse her beyond endurance.

"I need you inside me now," she gasped out.

"Come here." He cupped her shoulder, dragging her down against his body. "Let's see how well you rule," he murmured. "Put your legs on either side of my hips so you can slide me inside you."

She did as he asked, crying out as he filled her.

"Lean toward me a little," he asked, as she began to move.

When he took her breasts in his hands, heat welled within her. And as she moved above him, she felt them both climbing to a high peak of pleasure.

"So good. That's so good." His breath came in harsh gasps as she drove them both to ecstasy.

The sensations exploded, engulfing her in a firestorm of pleasure that consumed them both.

He called out her name, his hips rising as he emptied himself into her.

She collapsed onto his chest, breathing hard, feeling the pounding of her heart and his.

He stroked her shoulder, turning his head so that he could kiss her cheek.

"You're incredible," he whispered.

"With you," she answered. "Only with you. You've taught me so much about life in such a short time."

She allowed herself to relax for a few minutes, then lifted her head and looked at the clock on the backseat console. "Oh, Lord, we have to meet my father in an hour and a half. What's he going to think?"

"That you and I are going to be very happy together."

"But I must look like…"

He pushed back a damp strand of her blond hair. "Like you've been very thoroughly loved."

"I'm not supposed to do that before I marry."

"Hmm." He stroked his chin. "I think it's a little too late to get your virginity back."

"Be serious! In the palace we'll have to be discreet until we're married."

"Then I think we'll be taking some long rides in the country, because I'll go crazy if I'm living close to you without making love."

"I would, too. But I wouldn't have dared to do anything about it."

"Watch and learn."

She giggled, then climbed off him and began gathering up her clothing, still thinking about how she was going to look when she met her father.

Glancing up, she saw Shane gazing at her.

"Don't worry about getting ready for the king. I'm willing to bet the Beau Pays sapphire that there's a bathroom with a shower in that safe house. And a change of clothing for both of us."

When she breathed out a sigh, he gave her a broad grin. "But I can't guarantee that I'm not going to make love to you again in the shower."

She grinned back. "I heard the maids talk about doing that, too."

"Did you get all your sex instruction from the maids?"

"And a book my mother gave me. It was, uh, rather skimpy on the juicy details."

"Well, I think you're already doing a great job of filling in the blanks."

She finished pulling on her clothes, and so did he. And before they climbed out of the limousine, she gave him a soft kiss. "My father taught me how to serve my people. Thank you for teaching me how to be happy."

"We're just getting started, sweetheart. We're just getting started," he said, then gave her a questioning look. "Do you think your father would object if you took a week off in the States, getting instructions from your new security expert?"

She started to give him reasons why it wouldn't work, why she was too busy to take time off. But he plowed ahead. "Remember, you're supposed to be thinking differently. This is a combination of R & R and a working holiday at my state-of-the-art facility in the White Mountains."

"Right. Think differently," she murmured. "Yes, I believe the king will agree. Now that he knows I'm safe with you."

As they exited the car, she smiled at the man who had saved her life—in more ways than one. She knew she was the luckiest princess in the world. And she was going to remind herself of that every day for the rest of her life with this fantastic man.

* * * * *

THE ROYAL HOUSE OF NIROLI
Always passionate, always proud

The richest royal family in the world—united by blood and passion, torn apart by deceit and desire

Nestled in the azure blue of the Mediterranean Sea, the majestic island of Niroli has prospered for centuries. The Fierezza men have worn the crown with passion and pride since ancient times. But now, as the king's health declines, and his two sons have been tragically killed, the crown is in jeopardy.

The clock is ticking—a new heir must be found before the king is forced to abdicate. By royal decree the internationally scattered members of the Fierezza family are summoned to claim their destiny. But any person who takes the throne must do so according to The Rules of the Royal House of Niroli. Soon secrets and rivalries emerge as the descendents of this ancient royal line vie for position and power. Only a true Fierezza can become ruler—a person dedicated to their country, their people…and their eternal love!

Each month starting in July 2007,
Harlequin Presents is delighted to bring you
an exciting installment from
THE ROYAL HOUSE OF NIROLI,
in which you can follow the epic search
for the true Nirolian king.
Eight heirs, eight romances, eight fantastic stories!

Here's your chance to enjoy a sneak preview of the first book delivered to you by royal decree…

FIVE minutes later she was standing immobile in front of the study's window, her original purpose of coming in forgotten, as she stared in shocked horror at the envelope she was holding. Waves of heat followed by icy chill surged through her body. She could hardly see the address now through her blurred vision, but the crest on its left-hand front corner stood out, its *royal* crest, followed by the address: *HRH Prince Marco of Niroli...*

She didn't hear Marco's key in the apartment door, she didn't even hear him calling out her name. Her shock was so great that nothing could penetrate it. It encased her in a kind of bubble, which only concentrated the torment of what she was suffering and branded it on her brain so that it could never be forgotten. It was only finally pierced by the sudden opening of the study door as Marco walked in.

"Welcome home, *Your Highness*. I suppose I ought to curtsy." She waited, praying that he would laugh and tell her that she had got it all wrong, that the envelope she was holding, addressing him as Prince Marco of Niroli, was some silly mistake. But like a tiny candle flame shivering vulnerably in the dark, her hope trembled fearfully. And then the look in Marco's eyes extinguished it as cruelly as a hand placed callously over a dying person's face to stem their last breath.

"Give that to me," he demanded, taking the envelope from her.

"It's too late, Marco," Emily told him brokenly. "I know the truth now…." She dug her teeth in her lower lip to try to force back her own pain.

"You had no right to go through my desk," Marco shot back at her furiously, full of loathing at being caught off-guard and forced into a position in which he was in the wrong, making him determined to find something he could accuse Emily of. "I trusted you…."

Emily could hardly believe what she was hearing. "No, you didn't trust me, Marco, and you didn't trust me because you knew that I couldn't trust you. And you knew that because you're a liar, and liars don't trust people because they know that they themselves cannot be trusted." She not only felt sick, she also felt as though she could hardly breathe. "You are Prince Marco of Niroli…. How could you not tell me who you are and still live with me as intimately as we have lived together?" she demanded brokenly.

"Stop being so ridiculously dramatic," Marco demanded fiercely. "You are making too much of the situation."

"*Too much?*" Emily almost screamed the words at him. "When were you going to tell me, Marco? Perhaps you just planned to walk away without telling me anything? After all, what do my feelings matter to you?"

"Of course they matter." Marco stopped her sharply. "And it was in part to protect them, and you, that I decided not to inform you when my grandfather first announced that he intended to step down from the throne and hand it on to me."

"To protect me?" Emily nearly choked on her fury. "Hand on the throne? No wonder you told me when you first took me to bed that all you wanted was sex. You *knew* that was the only kind of relationship there could ever be between us! You *knew* that one day you would be Niroli's king. No doubt you are expected to marry a princess. Is she picked out for you already, your *royal* bride?"

* * * * *

Look for THE FUTURE KING'S PREGNANT
MISTRESS
by Penny Jordan in July 2007,
from Harlequin Presents,
available wherever books are sold.

Mission: Impassioned

A brand-new miniseries begins with

My Spy

By *USA TODAY* bestselling author

Marie Ferrarella

She had to trust him with her life....
It was the most daring mission of Joshua Lazlo's
career: rescuing the prime minister of England's
daughter from a gang of cold-blooded kidnappers.
But nothing prepared the shadowy secret agent
for a fiery woman whose touch ignited something
far more dangerous.

My Spy

#1472

Available July 2007 wherever you buy books!

nocturne™

**DON'T MISS THE RIVETING CONCLUSION
TO THE RAINTREE TRILOGY**

RAINTREE: SANCTUARY

by *New York Times* bestselling author

BEVERLY
BARTON

Mercy, guardian of the Raintree
homeplace, takes a stand against
the Ansara wizards to battle for
the Clan's future.

*On sale July,
wherever books are sold.*

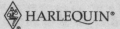

HARLEQUIN®
INTRIGUE®

COMING NEXT MONTH

#999 NAVAJO ECHOES by Cassie Miles
Bodyguards Unlimited, Denver, CO (Book 5 of 6)
Posing as newlyweds, agents John Pinto and Lily Clark escape to the Caribbean to put Prescott Personal Securities' biggest case to rest.

#1000 A BABY BEFORE DAWN by Linda Castillo
Lights Out (Book 2 of 4)
In the throes of a blackout, Chase Vickers will risk everything to rescue his lost love, a very pregnant Lily Garrett, from some very dangerous men seeking revenge.

#1001 24 KARAT AMMUNITION by Joanna Wayne
Four Brothers of Colts Run Cross
Eldest brother L.R. knows that all the oil money in the world won't make him happy if he can't rescue his first love and find out what made her run away from Texas so long ago.

#1002 THE NEW DEPUTY IN TOWN by B.J. Daniels
Whitehorse, Montana
Newly appointed sheriff Nick Rogers is hiding out in Montana from his murderous ex-partner. Despite adopting the local lifestyle, he's completely out of his realm, especially when being smitten with Laney Cavanaugh might blow his cover.

#1003 MIDNIGHT PRINCE by Dani Sinclair
When international playboy turned secret agent Reece Maddox teams with his mentor's daughter, will his secret identity be the only thing to unravel?

#1004 SPIRIT OF A HUNTER by Sylvie Kurtz
The Seekers
Dark and brooding Seeker Sabriel Mercer prefers to stick to the shadows. But when Nora Camden asks him to find her kidnapped son, the two will search the unforgiving White Mountains and find courage and love where least expected.

www.eHarlequin.com

HICNM0607